What About

Your Friends

A Novel

Teresa D. Patterson

What About Your Friends © 2010 by Teresa D. Patterson

Published by Edit Again Publications
Edit and layout by Teresa D. Patterson
Cover design by Teresa D. Patterson

Library of Congress Control Number: 2010936486

ISBN-13: 978-0-9826570-3-4

Email: editagainpublications@yahoo.com

Books by Teresa Patterson

*Project Queen
*Uncrossing Her Legs
*Ex-boyfriend
*In Need of a Joshua Man
*Spin Cycle

Dedication

To building friendships like pyramids.

Chapter One

Camille Gray gave up on the idea of sleeping. She fluffed the pillows and counted sheep, to no avail. She knew she'd never relax as long as she lay in the king-sized bed alone. Letting out a deep breath of frustration, she turned over and glanced at the clock. It was almost two in the morning and her husband, Dexter, still hadn't made it home. She had already called his cell phone repeatedly, leaving several messages.

What in the hell can he be doing at this time of night? Where is he? she thought. *Apparently, Dexter has better things to do than answer my calls.*

She conjured up an image of Dexter laid up with another woman. Picturing her husband screwing some trick made her blood boil.

"He better not do that to me," she said aloud. "He wouldn't."

Camille sat up and swung her legs over the side of the bed. She slid her feet into a pair of fluffy house shoes, got up and padded softly into the living room.

The light from the large-screened television illuminated the room. She didn't like the house to be dark when Dexter left her alone, so she left the TV on. She didn't feel safe by herself, but the noise from the television gave her a small amount of security. Maybe any potential burglars would hear it and think twice about breaking in.

A Judge Mathis re-run played on the screen. She sat down in the black leather love seat and picked up the remote

1

control. Just as she began channel surfing, she heard keys jangling outside the door.

Dexter stepped into the room only to encounter her cold glare. He glanced over at his wife, not saying a word. He was still dressed in the same clothes he wore to work. He had on dark slacks, a navy blue, long-sleeved shirt and silk tie.

Dexter was f-i-n-e. In fact, he was a Shemar Moore, Taye Diggs type of fine. He had it going on, with his caramel complexion and light-brown colored eyes. His looks definitely made him stand out.

Dexter immediately sensed that Camille had copped an attitude. He didn't feel like dealing with the same accusations that he'd dealt with all week. Sure that she would cut into him he headed toward the bedroom to avoid an argument.

Just as he'd expected, she began with the questions.

"Dexter, where have you been?" she demanded to know, suddenly standing on her feet.

Camille was all that and then some. She possessed a body that wouldn't quit. Her mocha colored skin was flawless. Her full breasts strained against the fabric of her gown. But, Dexter wasn't turned on by her looks. He had his guard up, especially since her eyes shot fire.

"This is the second time this week that you've come dragging your tired ass in after midnight. Do you have a damn problem?" she shouted.

"No, I do not have a problem," he answered calmly. "You must have one though, since you're the only one swearing and getting all loud." He continued past, but heard her stomping angrily behind him.

"Dexter, don't walk away from me when I'm talking to you. I've been calling you all night. Is something wrong with your phone? There must be since you can't seem to hear it ringing. Your dinner is cold and I've been up half the night worried about you. Where have you been?" Obviously, Dexter didn't intend to answer any of her questions. That made her hot. "Dexter!"

In the bedroom he stripped down to his boxers. Seeing him half-dressed conjured up an image of him in someone else's bedroom. Camille's blood ran hot. "Who the hell is she? What whore are you screwing? Are you cheating on me, Dexter? Is that it? Huh?" She glared at him with a wild look in her eyes, waiting for a response. She stood in the center of the room with her arms crossed.

"Camille, you're crazy," he said in annoyance. "Man, I don't have time for this. I have to work in the morning. I'm going to sleep." He had the audacity to climb into bed and turn his back on her. "Can you get the light?" he tossed over his shoulder.

That did it for her. It was the last straw. She rushed over to the bed, grabbed one of the pillows and let him have it.

"No, I will not get the fucking light!" She swung the pillow with all her might and hit him in the head. "And don't think that you're going to sleep in the same bed with me, you son-of-a-bitch! Take your ass to the couch."

"I swear you are tripping." He got up, shaking his head as he stared at her.

"I got a right to *trip*. I will not have you coming home whenever you feel like it. Did you forget that you have a wife? Did you forget your own address?" she yelled. Dexter offered no reply. "I guess you got amnesia and now you're mute, since you can't open your damn mouth."

"Look, I don't want to argue with you, Camille. I just don't, so I'm out," he said tiredly. He picked up his pillow and she watched as he left the room.

He remained so calm. Dexter was always the calm one. He didn't even slam the door; just let it close softly behind him.

Camille burst into tears. She sank down onto the carpeted floor and cried her heart out. She felt like she was riding an emotional roller coaster, up one minute, down the next.

Does marriage only consist of this? she thought.

Married for four, short months, her marriage seemed to already be headed for disaster. She knew that picking a fight would not solve their problems. Dexter just made her so mad. Plus, he never wanted to talk things out. He said she always made too much out of small things. He acted like nothing mattered to him at all. She often wondered what went on inside his head and his heart. Didn't he want to be with her?

Dexter was the one who'd insisted that they get married right away. She wanted to wait in order to be sure.

Camille finally got up off the floor and walked over to the mirror. She placed her hands on her protruding stomach and gazed at her image. She'd been pregnant for almost five months. She thought that she wanted a baby with Dexter. Now doubt and uncertainty set in.

Dexter insisted that he hadn't married her only because of the pregnancy, but she wasn't so sure about that. He didn't seem to want to be around her anymore. He worked more hours and came home late the past few weeks.

Camille sighed. She just didn't know what to think. She knew that she loved Dexter. She'd loved him on first sight. But, could that kind of love be the lasting kind? Would their marriage endure the many trials and tribulations ahead and sustain?

She couldn't continue with such a rift existing between them. She had to get Dexter to communicate. She prayed for answers, but knew they wouldn't materialize out of thin air.

She got a tissue and dabbed at her red-rimmed eyes, blew her nose, then threw the tissue in the small garbage can near the dresser. Camille ran her fingers through her thick, shoulder length hair and sighed, tiredly. Suddenly, a light seemed to click on inside her head.

"That's it," she said aloud. A makeover. She would go to the beauty salon and get her hair styled. She would also treat herself to a manicure and a pedicure. Then, she would find a j-o-b.

For the past two months, she had been so wrought with morning sickness that the doctors placed her on bed rest. She'd been so sick that water wouldn't even stay down. Consequently, she had to quit her job at the department store located in the mall. She couldn't continue working there due to having to stand up all day. Dexter's paycheck provided the only source of income. That could be the reason for his sullen mood.

Dexter would never ask her to get a job. It wasn't his way. Dexter was born and raised in Philadelphia. He portrayed the ideal picture of the perfect husband: handsome, hardworking, a provider. He believed strongly in family values. If Camille didn't watch herself, she could turn into one of those barefoot, pregnant women. She made a promise to herself she'd never fit that mode.

She assumed that having to foot all of the bills contributed to Dexter's stress. He wouldn't talk to her about it because of his stubborn, male pride. He felt that a man should provide for his family.

Now that the severe morning sickness had ended, she could find no valid reason as to why she shouldn't work.

Yeah, getting a job would do the trick. Camille would become employed, and take some of the strain off her husband. Maybe that would help put their marriage back on track.

She smiled to herself, already feeling optimistic. Soon, the real Camille would be back full force. Suddenly, she felt like dancing. She even felt good enough to satisfy her man.

She let her mind drift back and couldn't believe that a month had passed since she and Dexter made love. No wonder the brother acted so uptight. Newlyweds should make love every night.

She didn't actually believe that he cheated with another woman, as she'd accused earlier, but she wasn't stupid either. She knew that if she didn't give her husband the attention that he needed in the bedroom, some low-morale chicken-head out there would.

Camille pulled her hair back into a ponytail and got into bed. She missed having Dexter's warmth next to her, but he could stay on the couch. He made her sick with his nonchalant attitude. The last time he stayed out late, he didn't have a good explanation either.

She tried to forget about everything and let go of the anger. She realized that she felt better than she'd felt in a while. She had a plan that she would put into effect tomorrow. She just prayed it would work because she didn't want her marriage to end. The arguing and getting nowhere with Dexter made her tired. A light had to be waiting at the end of the tunnel.

Chapter Two

*T*he next morning Camille got up bright and early. By the time Dexter showered and dressed, she had breakfast on the table. Blueberry pancakes, sausage patties and bacon, grits, toast and orange juice greeted him. Folgers brewed in the glass coffeepot and Camille appeared presentable. When he entered the room, he did a double-take.

"Is this real?" he asked aloud, so used to seeing her looking tore up, leaning over the toilet bowl or still in the bed. He was taken aback seeing his wife actually dressed. She had styled her hair and even wore a dab of lipstick. "Whoa."

"Good morning," she greeted, unable to quite meet his eyes. Her behavior from the night before caused her to be thoroughly ashamed. She had no reason to hurl such vile accusations at her husband, whom she truly loved. A fresh wave of guilt washed over her. "Dexter, I'm sorry for the way that I've been acting," she said tearfully. "It's just that- I worry about you when you don't come home. I don't expect for you to call every hour and check in or anything, but it would be nice if you would just let me know when you're going to be late," she told him. "It's common courtesy."

He looked at her struggling to hold back the tears and it touched his heart. "Baby, I'm sorry too," he said thickly. "I haven't made things easy for you. It's just that when I leave in the morning- you're sick. When I come home in the evening- you're sick. When I want to get freaky- you're sick." He gazed at her with compassion. "I guess I haven't been very understanding. I apologize. I just didn't know that it would be like this," he ended.

7

"Me either," she said quietly. "But, I don't want to lose you, Dexter." Her eyes bore into his. "I love you. You are my life."

"Camille, don't start getting all emotional on me. I'm your husband. I'm not going anywhere. I'll always be here for you and our baby." He sat down and began eating, ending the discussion.

It didn't go unnoticed by Camille that he hadn't said he loved her. Had he ever said it?

She thought back on their short relationship. She knew Dexter for only six months before she found out she was pregnant. Even though instant love happened for her, she wasn't sure of Dexter's true feelings. He told her that he wanted to spend the rest of his life with her. He also told her that she'd finally found someone whom she could love. But he'd never, not once, actually said those three words to her.

"Dexter," she said softly and he looked up from eating.

"Yes?"

"Do you love me?" she asked, holding his gaze.

An annoyed scowl crossed his handsome face. "Camille, what kind of a question is that? I married you, didn't I?" He reached for another pancake. "Breakfast is great, Baby. Thank you."

"No problem," she said stiffly.

Camille got up from the table. She felt heaviness in her heart and her throat constricted. It wasn't exactly the response she'd expected. But that was Dexter- so unemotional.

"Since you're up, could you pour me a cup of coffee?" he asked, grabbing the newspaper that she'd placed on the table earlier.

"Pour it your damn self," she snapped and left the room.

Dexter's head raised and a look of confusion flashed across his face. He watched her back as she stalked out. The door to their bedroom slammed shut.

"Damn. What did I do now?" he wondered aloud. He shook his head and turned to the sports section. He found it hard to figure Camille out. One minute she would be up, the next, down. He contributed it to her being pregnant. He wouldn't let her mood swings bother him, though. She had gone all out and cooked a wonderful breakfast. He couldn't complain about that at all.

He kept reading the paper until the clock on the wall read 7:15. He placed his dishes in the sink then left for work.

When Camille went back into the kitchen Dexter wasn't there. He hadn't said "good-bye," hadn't given her a kiss. Nothing. The only thing he'd left her was a messed up kitchen.

She shook her head as she scraped the remaining food down the garbage disposal and placed the dishes into the dishwasher. She cleaned the rest of the kitchen and even carried out the garbage.

Camille decided to job search, so she got the classified section of the newspaper that still lay on the table. After scanning the advertisements under clerical and general employment, she narrowed it down to two positions that matched her skills and qualifications.

She dialed the number to the first ad she'd circled, and cradled the cordless phone between her shoulder and jaw as she walked over to the coffee pot. Since finding out about her pregnancy, she'd stopped drinking caffeine. She couldn't successfully give up coffee, but now she drank only decaffeinated.

"Good morning, Dr. Raphael's office," a cheerful voice greeted from the other end of the phone.

"Good morning, ma'am. I'm calling to inquire about the secretarial position in today's paper."

"Oh, I'm sorry. We filled that position yesterday," the woman told her. Her voice held genuine regret. "But thank you for calling."

"Thank you." She hung up feeling somewhat disappointed, but not discouraged.

She got ready to dial the next number when her eye caught an ad at the top of the page that she'd missed. A temporary employment agency advertised for clerical workers. They had a variety of job positions, both full and part-time.

Maybe a temporary position would be better, with her being pregnant and all. If she didn't like working one of the assignments, she could always pass it up. If she did like any of the jobs, maybe she would consider becoming a permanent employee once she'd given birth. She had many options. Feeling optimistic, she dialed the number.

She agreed to a two o'clock appointment later that evening at the temp agency. She would fill out the necessary paperwork and do testing for typing and data entry. That left her plenty of time to get a manicure and have her hair styled. She wanted to make a good first impression.

She printed out a copy of her resume that had been saved on the C drive of her computer. She placed it in an attractive resume folder, and put that inside her briefcase. Not knowing how long it would take at the beauty salon, she took everything that she needed with her.

When she left the house, she was dressed to impress. She wore a black, two-pieced pants suit. She tied a black and white zebra striped scarf around her neck and slipped her feet into matching, open-toed sandals with heels. In her business wear, she didn't even appear to be pregnant.

She arrived at Intrigue Hair Design a quarter past ten. Patrick, the male hair stylist worked on doing a sew-in for one of his customers. He informed that he could have her out around noon. Once he finished sewing the older woman's hair and hot curled it, Camille would be next in the chair.

She picked up a *Black Hair* magazine and thumbed through it. As she waited, the manicurist came in and set up her workstation.

"Excuse me, are you booked up today?" Camille asked.

"Naw, girl. You want your nails done?" the cherub-faced girl asked. Camille nodded. "You can sit down here." She indicated the chair in front of her manicurist table. Camille took a seat.

"Is it possible to get a pedicure too?"

"Yeah, girl. No problem."

For the next hour she got hooked up. Her feet were soaked, oiled, and massaged. She received a French manicure and pedicure. Finally, she sat in the styling chair.

"You know what kind of style you want?" Patrick, a handsome, brown-skinned, young man with pretty eyes asked. He was dressed in Sean Jean gear and smelled really nice. Camille could almost bet it was Joop cologne, but she wasn't sure

"Yes, I want something easy to manage, like a Bob cut."

"You're going to let me cut off all of your long, pretty hair?" he exclaimed. "Are you sure that's what you want me to do?" he asked.

"Yes. I need a change," Camille told him. "I'm ready," she said with conviction.

"Okay. But, don't be crying when I start cutting." He had a sense of humor and a pleasant aura. She liked him right off. She felt for certain that she'd found herself a permanent hair stylist.

When Patrick finished, her swiveled the chair around so she could see the ending results. She stared at her reflection in amazement. He'd transformed her hair into a medium length, stylish Bob. It accented her beautiful, mahogany colored skin tone. She even had him arch her eyebrows, which made her appear exotic. She felt confident and self-assured. She gave both Patrick and the nail technician a generous tip and headed to her interview.

Camille had no problems taking the tests. Even with her new nail tips she could type over seventy words per minute and 10,000 keystrokes. Her professionalism and test scores greatly impressed the agency.

Camille's accomplishments of the day pleased her. She stopped by Winn Dixie Supermarket and purchased T-bone steaks, a couple of baking potatoes and the fixings for a Caesar salad. She had some corn on the cob in the freezer at home. That would give the meal an added touch.

As she drove towards home it dawned on her that she was actually happy. She'd felt down and depressed for so long that it felt good to have the dark cloud lifted. She was determined not to let anything spoil her mood. If Dexter came home late, she wasn't going to go off on him. She would just accept it. She had to begin controlling her temper. If not, it would, inevitably, drive Dexter away.

Once home, she changed out of her interview clothes and began to prepare dinner. She seasoned the steaks and placed them on the George Foreman grill, one of the gifts she received at her wedding shower. She loved her George Foreman gill. It made grilling meats so easy and quick.

She wrapped the potatoes in aluminum foil and placed them in the oven. Getting the corn on the cob out of the freezer, she placed them in a pot of boiling, salted water. Next, she mixed the Caesar salad.

Once she'd prepared everything, she set the table. She pulled out the fancy tablecloth and placemats that they only used for special occasions. She even put a candle in the center of the table. She wanted Dexter to be surprised. Camille hadn't shown him any affection for quite some time. Tonight that would change.

Amazingly, Dexter stepped through the door at a little after five thirty. Once again, he received a shock.

"Damn! You hooked it up," she heard, while in the bedroom room getting ready to make her grand entrance. "Camille, where are you?" he called.

"Just a minute," she called back. She took a deep breath and entered the room. "Hello," she said in what she hoped to be a seductive tone. Dexter turned around and his eyes widened. Then, his mouth dropped open.

Camille wore a red, sheer negligee. It had imitation feathers around the low-cut collar. The sheer robe had feathers at the cuffs of the sleeves. She wore tiny, matching g-string panties underneath.

"Good Lawd!" Dexter exclaimed. "I guess dinner can wait. I see something far more appetizing." He walked over and embraced her. "You look so beautiful," he told her in regards to her transformation. He lightly touched her new hairstyle. "Nice. I like it." She smiled at the compliment, pleased. She'd been a bit nervous about the change but now knew that she'd made the right decision.

Dexter lowered his head and captured her lips with his own. He kissed her passionately. Her heart pounded rapidly in her chest.

Dexter's hands began to explore, caressing the places on her body that had filled out because of pregnancy. She felt the heat through the thin material of the gown. He grasped her bare buttocks in his strong hands. "Oh baby," he moaned, deepening the kiss between them.

"I've missed you," she breathed passionately, "so much."

"Well, let's take care of that," he said and lifted her up into his arms. He carried her to the bedroom and placed her gently on the bed.

Dexter removed the robe. Camille's breast strained against the flimsy lingerie, bulging over the top. Her nipples stood hard and erect. He bent his head and gently sucked on each of them.

Camille closed her eyes and enjoyed the intense pleasure that her husband delivered. Her love-starved body caused her to moan like a wanton hussy and beg Dexter to enter her. She didn't want to wait for foreplay. She felt close to explosion.

Dexter quickly obliged her. He undressed swiftly and parted her thighs. He touched her moistness with his middle and index finger. She sobbed from the pleasure.

"Dexter, please," she begged.

Dexter's excitement increased. He couldn't remember a time that Camille showed such eagerness to make love. Her reaction stimulated him. He rose above her and eased forward. She felt so warm and soft. He felt her muscles tighten around his erection. She squeezed and released. Squeezed and released. It drove him so wild that his ejaculation surged from him. He pushed deeper and deeper into her hot flesh. He could feel the insides of her walls tremble and shiver, vibrate and contract as she reached orgasm.

Wave after wave of pleasure washed over Camille. She screamed out and rose to meet him, thrust for thrust. Then, she experienced another intense climax that left her shaking. Dexter held her until she finally lay still. Their breaths came in ragged spurts. Her brown skin glistened with perspiration. Sweat poured from his golden body.

Dexter gazed into her eyes and saw the love within their depths. There was no way that he'd be able to tell her what lay heavily on his heart. He couldn't reveal to her that he'd met someone who could cause problems for them. Not now and maybe never. He knew she wouldn't understand.

The guilt ate away at him as he rolled off of her, careful not to touch the small bulge in her stomach. He got up and went to take a shower.

After showering and changing they sat down to eat dinner. Dexter wore a pair of paisley, silk boxers with a matching robe. Camille had on a short, white, silk gown with a robe that tied in the front.

"How was your day?" she asked, slicing into her medium-well done steak. She took a bite and closed her eyes to savor the flavor.

"Tough," he told her, smiling slightly at her blissful expression. "But in construction, that's the way it is."

Camille didn't mind that Dexter had a blue-collar job. In her opinion, Dexter was the greatest. She couldn't picture him in a corporate environment. Being behind a desk and a computer wasn't his style. Plus, he loved his job and made a lot of money doing what he did.

He'd served in the Army for six years, but decided against pursing a military career. The military and living in foster homes had put a rough edge to him. The Army and his adoptive father shaped him into the man that he'd become.

She knew the Grays weren't Dexter's biological parents, but he talked about them as if they had raised him from birth. He had an abundance of love and great respect for the Grays.

Back when they'd dated, he revealed that his biological mother gave him up for adoption. He never mentioned wanting to locate her, so Camille left the subject alone. Despite the fact that he'd dealt with a lot of issues as a child, Dexter turned out to be a phenomenal human being.

She stared at him across the table, pride shining in her eyes.

"I have something to tell you." She passed him the sour cream for his baked potato. "I might start working again next week."

Dexter paused from spooning sour cream onto his potato. "Oh?" His brow lifted.

"Yes. I went to a temp agency. They said they'd call me with a job assignment next week," she said excitedly.

"Well, Camille, I don't know about this," he said slowly, not wanting to dampen her spirits. "The doctor said you should take it easy."

"Dexter, I'm over all of my morning sickness. I feel fine. Besides, we need the money. I know that it can't be easy for you paying all of the bills around here."

"Camille, you don't need to worry about that," he stated, beginning to get a little agitated. Camille had yet to learn to let a man be a man. If he didn't mind handling all the finances, she should just accept it.

"I know," she said quickly, picking up on his aggravation. "I just figured that I could help out financially and it would take some of the strain off of you."

"Strain?" He stopped eating and stared at her. "Is that what you think is wrong?"

"Well, yes. I can't think of any other reason for you to be so distant," she told him.

She was so naïve, which wasn't a bad thing. But, sometimes, he wondered if she had blonde roots. He could think of several reasons that he'd been so distant. Reason number one: she'd pushed him away with her constant nagging. Reason number two, he didn't like to argue so he stayed away from home as much as possible. He could go on and on, but he wouldn't dare open his mouth and tell her. She'd just get mad and give him another reason to add to the list.

"Maybe you're right," he lied. He knew damn well that he wasn't under any financial strain. He owned a construction company and managed an entire construction crew. He made a net income of over a hundred thousand dollars per year. He didn't have the heart to tell her the main reason for his lack of focus and attention. He'd wait until she got through the pregnancy. He'd be able to tell her then. He just didn't know how long he could keep quiet about Meredith.

He wished he'd never taken that woman to lunch from day one. It wouldn't matter to Camille that Meredith was his secretary. She would have a fit and accuse him of cheating. He couldn't stand when she did that. It made him think about doing what she accused him of.

Dexter gazed at his wife as thoughts ran through his mind. Camille was wonderful. She was beautiful on the inside and out. In his heart, he really loved her. Nevertheless, he sometimes felt like he'd moved too fast. He never should have married Camille. He wasn't really ready for marriage.

Who was he trying to fool? If he had a solid marriage, he wouldn't feel an attraction to Meredith. He wouldn't have let the thought of cheating on his wife enter into his head or his heart.

Dexter felt obligated to make things right when Camille got pregnant. After all, it was entirely his fault. He never doubted that the baby belonged to him. He was the only man that Camille had ever slept with. She was a rarity: a twenty-two year old virgin. Her innocence was one of the characteristics that drew him to her.

Dexter had to do the right thing. He missed out on growing up in a two-parent home until the Gray's took him in. He felt it took both a mother and a father to raise a child that would become a productive member of society. He would never be one of those absent fathers on the channel 28 News's Deadbeat Dad's segment. His child would be raised with values and morals that only two parents could instill. He would be there for his child from birth until death. Just as he would be there for his wife "until death do us part."

Lately, Meredith made it hard for him to honor his marriage vows. Meredith could be the "strain" on his marriage. He couldn't tell Camille that, though. He had to deal with Meredith on his own and in a manner that wouldn't destroy his wife. He knew Camille's whole world revolved around him, and he didn't want her hurt.

As he continued to eat, he actually considered the thought of her working. It might not be such a bad idea. Maybe she would find some friends, someone she could relate to. At first, it flattered him that she considered him her everything. But, now it almost stifled him.

"Honey, do you want another piece of corn on the cob?" Camille's voice interrupted his thoughts.

"Er- sure. I'll take another," he finally answered.

She stared at him, curiously. "You were lost in your thoughts. Anything you'd like to talk about? Something bothering you?" she questioned.

"No, Baby. Nothing at all," he said, avoiding her gaze. "Well, dinner was wonderful," he told her.

"I actually enjoyed what took place before dinner," she said softly.

Her confession brought a smile to his face. He could feel his desire return full force as he thought about their heated session of love-making hours before.

"I could use some dessert," he told her suggestively. "What about you?"

Camille blushed and giggled like a schoolgirl. "Whatever makes you happy sweetheart." She got up, walked over and sat on his lap. She stared into his light brown eyes. "I love you." She didn't wait for a response, just placed her lips on his and slipped her tongue into his mouth.

Her boldness shocked Dexter. He was usually the aggressive one. Camille remained shy and reserved when it came to sex. But at the moment, she took full control. She ran her slender, soft hands down his back. She gently clawed at him with her fingernails and Dexter groaned.

Camille straddled him in the chair. She kissed his earlobes and neck, going lower. She let her delicate tongue encircle his nipple and she sucked and licked until Dexter thought she would blow his mind. She went lower, kneading his shoulders and chest with her small hands as she kissed his navel. She licked the inside of his belly button causing him to moan. She pinched both of his nipples gently as she received him into her hot mouth.

"Oh, baby," Dexter moaned, as she slipped her lips over him. She caressed him with her hands as she sucked and licked. She had never done this sexual act before and it amazed Dexter at how good she was at it. "Camille." He called her name. "That feels so good."

She engaged in foreplay for a while longer then stood up, letting the robe and gown fall to the floor. Slowly, she straddled Dexter once again and eased her moistness down onto his shaft. Dexter throbbed with the weight of his erection. As Camille moved, he gripped her buttocks tightly. She rode him like a thoroughbred. Just when he thought he would burst, he felt her muscles tighten as she climaxed. She cried out and fell against his chest, holding on for dear life as she trembled and shook. Dexter let loose. He exploded like a volcano. It was the best sex they'd experienced since getting married.

Chapter Three

April Dillard paced the floor of her apartment. She was furious. Her two children, ages seven and eleven months, bickered, as usual. Her head ached because she was sick and tired of yelling at them. It did no good anyway. She felt frustrated and blamed Darren, her son's father. He had promised to pick up Darren Jr. earlier that day. Of course, it was almost two o'clock in the evening and he still hadn't arrived.

That no good bastard she fumed inside. She always had to beg him for help. He barely supported his son financially because he wouldn't keep a job. The least he could do was pick him up every other weekend. He slacked all the time. He got DJ once a month or he picked him up on a Friday night and brought him back on Saturday.

She considered putting him on child support and to hell with it. She could care less if he saw his son or not. She thought it was so lame that some deadbeat fathers out there wouldn't support their kids, but cried blood the minute they were ordered to do so by a court.

She didn't know whether or not Darren would be one of those deadbeats, but she'd reached the point of not caring. She was fed up. Darren made her sick. He only acted so irresponsibly when he got back with his girlfriend. When he lived with his mama, he got DJ for the entire weekend.

April didn't know what to do. Sometimes she would sit and cry about her situation. At twenty-three, she was a single parent with two children. Her daughter's father recently became involved in her life. On the flipside, he decreased the amount of his child support payments. He had better things to do with his money, like buy new rims for his sporty BMW.

April loved her children, but sometimes they stressed her out and she needed a break. She got relief when she went clubbing. She couldn't go out if she didn't have someone to watch the kids. Her mother used to baby-sit for her, but began working a new job and didn't get off until late. Sometimes, she would still watch the kids, but not often.

April wanted to go to Ybor City. A group of her co-workers agreed to meet up and hang out on Saturday. In Ybor, anybody could find something to do. Several nightclubs populated the main strip. She wanted to hang, get drunk, and forget about her problems.

If Darren didn't pick up DJ, she'd be home yet another weekend. The thought depressed her.

She had the mini blinds opened and could see Darren finally pull up in a black Nissan, his girlfriend's car, no doubt. She glanced over at the children. They had finally settled down to watch the Cartoon Network. She opened the door to confront him before he had a chance to knock.

"Why the hell are you so late?" she yelled. Darren just grinned and looked down.

"You know how it is. I don't have transpo. So, I have to get him when I can," he explained, still grinning.

That's what made her so angry. He thought everything was a joke.

"See. That's what pisses me off about you," she told him. "You think everything is so damn funny. I got a car. I could have dropped him off and you know that," she snapped.

"Well, where my lil' man at," he asked, changing the subject.

"In the damn house."

"Go get him. Hurry up. I gotta get this car back."

"Why? It must belong to ya bitch? Is that why you tryin'
to rush off?"

"Man, it ain't even like that," he denied.

"Whatever!" She went back inside and he followed her
into the bedroom.

Darren came up behind her while she tried to get DJ's
things together.

"Damn girl, don't bend over like that," he said, chuckling
as he pressed himself up against the back of her.

"Don't even think about it," she warned, straightening up
and moving away from him.

"April, stop tripping. You know I get him when I can.
Give a brother a break."

"You don't give me a damn break!" She was unrelenting.

"You always have to give me attitude when I come over
here. Man, that ain't even cool."

Darren was an immature twenty-two-year old and it
showed. He had no sense of responsibility. He didn't know
the first thing about being a parent.

"Darren, I'm sick of this," she told him. "You should get
him every other weekend. It's not like you give me money.
You don't pay daycare. You don't buy him clothes or shoes.
You should be happy to get him to make up for not providing
for him financially."

"You know I ain't working right now. But, that's gonna
change. I'm gonna do better."

"When?" she asked sarcastically. She didn't believe him.
She grew tired of staring into his lying face. "When he's
eighteen and don't need you?" She threw DJ's overnight bag
at him. "Just take him and go."

"Man, why you tripping?" He picked up the bag, which had fallen on the floor and headed to the living room.

"And he needs some Pull Ups, too," she called behind him.

April stayed in the room for a few minutes in order to calm down. Darren wasn't the best father, but at least he did try. Even though she felt he could do much better, she appreciated his efforts. However, she wasn't going to tell him that because if she did, he would probably feel that he could continue to slack instead of show improvement. She wished he'd get a job and keep it for more than a few months.

She went into the living room. Darren had switched from the Cartoon Network to B.E.T and they all danced to rap videos. It brought a small smile to her face that she tried to hide, but Darren caught it.

"Hey Peaches," he called her daughter, Alexis, by her nickname, "Look. Do this." He did some crazy dance that Peaches imitated to a tee. "You go ' head!"

DJ tried to dance too. They played around for a few minutes until Darren remembered the time.

"Hey, I got to go," Darren said. Without warning, he grabbed April and kissed her. The kids cracked up laughing as she tried to push him away. "When I bring him back tomorrow night, can we hook up?" he whispered in her ear.

"No."

"Come on. Stop playing hard to get. You want me. You not gonna hook me up?"

She pushed at his chest, and turned her head when he tried to kiss her again.

"Darren, go away," she said, half-heartedly. It was so hard to resist him. He was her son's father and she still had strong feelings for him. She didn't want to be second in his life and Darren just didn't want to do right.

"Well, when I bring him back just be ready," he told her. He was so confident of himself. He knew that he looked good and had charm, which drove women crazy. She was not excluded because she'd fallen for him too.

He got DJ's bag and picked DJ up. "Tell ya mama bye," he told him.

"Bye-bye," DJ said in his childish voice, waving at his mother and sister.

Finally, Darren left and she breathed a sigh of relief. Now she could relax.

"Peaches, I'm taking you over to Grandma's. I'm going out tonight," she told her daughter.

"Aw man! Why I always gotta go over there?" she pouted. "Why can't I stay here?"

"Because I said that you're going over to Grandma's. Don't start with me, Peaches," she told her.

"Man, whatever!"

"Don't get hit in the mouth," April warned.

"I'll call 911 and I'll tell them too," she sassed. Peaches stared at her mother, as if daring her to follow through on her threat.

"You got a lot of mouth for a seven year old. Now shut up and go pack some clothes because you're spending the night."

After dropping Peaches off at her mother's, April met her co-workers in the parking lot of the insurance company where they worked. It took them a while to decide whose car they would take and who would be the designated driver. April made sure that it wasn't her. She never liked to be the designated driver; that would mean that she couldn't get her drink on the way she wanted to. Plus, she didn't want a bunch of drunkards throwing up in her car. Co-workers or not, she would have a real problem with that.

In the end, Katie drove. Katie was wild. Rumor had it that she'd slept with every available man at the job, even the new manager. April wondered how Katie had managed to do that, if the rumor held any truth. Their manager Brad was too fine. She wouldn't mind hooking up with him herself. Katie was easy and she tried everybody's man. April liked her, but she didn't trust the heifer one bit.

Katie used drugs and April didn't like that either. She liked to "roll" which meant she did X-tasy. April wanted no part of that. Now, she would smoke a joint every now and then, but when it came to that other stuff, she opted out.

No sooner as they pulled into a gas station to get gas and beer, Katie took out a bag of pills.

"Hey, April, want to try one?" she offered. "Any of you guys?" she asked, looking at the other three.

"Hell no," April refused. Everyone else declined as well.

Katie got out and went inside to get bottled water.

"What the hell is her problem?" Jessica asked. "Is she taking drugs? I had no idea that she did that shit." Jessica looked shocked.

"Hey, it's cool. She can handle it," Paul told her. "She does it all the time."

"Well, why didn't anybody tell me? I sure as hell wouldn't be riding in a car with her. This shit is fucked up."

"Yeah it is," April agreed. "We'll go this time, but next time, somebody else is driving." Everyone went into the store to get alcoholic beverages.

They arrived in Ybor around eleven o'clock. It took a while to find a place to park because of the congested streets filled with all of the club hoppers. At twenty minutes after eleven, they finally found a spot.

Walking down the strip was a party in itself. They encountered all types of people. Some dressed up, and others wore almost nothing. April got a lot of calls and it felt good. She always wore short dresses or skirts with high heels. She didn't like pants. She stood five feet two and had long, dark hair, which was wavy and thick. A perm wouldn't straighten it for long. This could be attributed to the fact that she was bi-racial. She had an African American father and a Caucasian mother. She was very pretty, but not conceited. She rated herself as average. She felt overweight because of having two children and getting the Depo Provera shot administered every three months. However, the men in Ybor had no complaints.

The group went to a club called The Empire where they advertised two for one drinks. April noticed that the crowded club held a majority of white people. Neon lights flashed. Cages adorned the place and women and men gyrated around inside them. April felt good enough to be bold after about fifteen minutes of steady drinking. She got in one of the cages and danced with a black guy. He looked at her like she was crazy, turned his back and started dancing with a white girl. April didn't know what his problem was, but she wasn't going to let it get to her. She kept dancing. Katie got in the cage with Vu Lee, an Asian guy who had a crush on her and every female he encountered. He was still a virgin at age twenty-one. He tried so hard to get laid, but it never worked. No one wanted to get involved with a guy that stood about four feet eight.

Katie was all over Vu. You couldn't tell if she was drunk or high from the pills; probably both. She started to do the "booty dance." The guys around got quickly excited. They wanted a free show, so they cheered her on. From the looks of it she floated on cloud nine.

It wasn't long before April got bored with the crowd. The rest of the crew was close to being wasted because they'd stayed near the bar. It amazed April at how much liquor they all could consume, her included. The drunken group would probably agree to anything so she told them she wanted to check out another club. Soon they left and headed down the strip again.

They stood in a line to get into the Full Moon Saloon. When they entered, April could tell that this club was more her style. The people were a mixture of black, white and Hispanic. It was a medium sized club with plenty of areas to dance. People danced on the floor, on the stage, and in another roofless area. A major radio station broadcasted live and the station was wild. The popular DJ from the morning show got on the microphone and made an announcement.

"We're asking all of you fly ladies, who know that you got it going on to get on the bar and show it off. Any lady that gets on the bar and dance will get free shots and a chance to win a Party Package. Also," he paused for effect. "The first lady to show off her thong-" the men in the crowd cheered loud and excitedly, drowning the DJ out. "Like I said, the first lady to show off the best thong will win $100. The runner up will get $50."

It didn't take long for the bar to fill up. About ten women got up on the bar to dance and show off their thongs. The men piled up to the bar, waving dollars and trying to feel the women's legs. Some of them even went further, groping the women in private spots. The majority of the drunken women didn't care.

April ordered another Hennessy and Coke. By then, her head spun. They played her song, a popular number featuring Snoop Dogg. She waved her hands in the air, bounced around with the rest of the crowd and chanted the lyrics aloud. All of her troubles got cast to the back of her mind, for the time being.

***

April awoke around one o'clock Sunday afternoon with a pounding headache. She didn't want to get up but had promised her mother she'd pick up Peaches. She couldn't leave her at her parent's house because her mom had to be at work at three. Asking her brother to baby-sit was out of the question. Otis had issues. He needed anger management.

After picking Peaches up they went to McDonald's because April didn't feel like cooking. Besides, she'd run out of just about everything and didn't have any grocery money. Her child support check from Peaches' father hadn't come. A few weeks before, she had received the news that he wanted to lower his child support payments. He only paid $60 a week as it was and she always received that late. She was going to do whatever she could to make him continue to pay the measly $60 a week. After all, he had just decided to become a part of his daughter's life. April thought that his wife had masterminded the whole thing. She couldn't stand her phony, ugly behind. Plus, his wife must be stupid if she thought that her husband didn't still have doggish ways.

Less than an hour after she returned home, Darren called.

"I need for you to come and get 'im," he told her.

"Why? I'm not ready to get him yet. You can't bring him later?"

"Naw, I got something to do."

"Did you get him some Pull Ups?" Silence came from the on the other end. "Darren, you heard me, did you buy him some Pull Ups?"

"Er- naw. I forget," he finally said.

"Well, you need to get him some or give me the money to get them. I'm broke."

"I'll get some, but you have to come get him now," Darren bribed.

"I'll be there in about fifteen minutes," she told him, reluctantly.

April jerked awake. She couldn't figure out where the persistent sound came from. She hit the alarm clock but the sound continued. Her cell phone rang with a relentless buzz. When she finally figured it out, she grabbed it and answered.

"Hello?"

"Hey, what's up?" the voice on the other end said.

"Who is this?"

"This Darius. You met me at the club the other night," he explained.

April searched her mind trying to place the face with the name, but couldn't. Hell, she had gotten sloppy drunk. She had no idea whom she'd given her number to.

"Well, I was sleep," she mumbled. She looked at the clock on the nightstand. 5:45. He had interrupted her sleep at that time of morning. She decided that she already didn't like him.

"Don't you have to go to work?" he asked.

"Yeah, but I don't have to get up until seven. I'll call you back later."

"Okay. Bye."

"Damn!" She could kick herself for giving out her number. She wished she'd turned her cell phone off. What in the hell had possessed him to call her so early in the morning? Now, she'd never get back to sleep.

"Who was that?" Darren's voice boomed in the darkness. So, he'd awakened and decided to listen to her conversation.

"None of your damn business," she snapped. She was upset with him and with herself for giving in. "Get your ass up and go home."

"So, it's like that now?" Darren sat up in bed. "Man, you always tripping." He got out of bed and began pulling on his clothes.

April tried to go back to sleep but thoughts of the previous night kept running through her head.

She'd gone to pick up DJ and Darren had stood by the car as she buckled DJ into his car seat.

"So, can I come by later tonight?" he asked, staring her up and down.

"No."

"Come on. I just want to talk. I think we should be together because of DJ. We need to work things out."

April felt her heart softening. All she ever wanted was for Darren to do right and be a permanent part of their lives. She didn't want to be his booty call or play second to his girlfriend of the moment.

"Well, okay, but we're going to talk, nothing else," she told him, getting into the car. He smiled, leaned into the window and gave her a kiss.

"I'll see you later."

Darren arrived at ten and at first they had talked. He reminded her of the reason they'd broken up in the first place.

They were both so young. April wasn't sure if she really loved Darren. She liked being with him because of his looks. That didn't mean she loved him.

While she dated him, she'd met someone else. She and the other guy began a relationship. The other guy ended up going to jail for a felony charge. While locked up, he insisted that she break up with Darren, in order to prove that she loved him. She felt so confused. When you're young, you don't really know for sure what you want. She thought that she'd done the right thing at the time.

Now, she knew she'd made the wrong choice. Breaking up with Darren had only caused problems. The other man had been out of her life and out of prison for a long time.

"When you chose that lame duck over me, it hurt me bad," Darren told her. "I don't know if I can ever get over that."

"I made a mistake," she said.

All of the guilt rushed back. She remembered the day it happened. Darren cried like a baby. He begged her not to break up with him and she did it anyway. "It's all in the past."

"But how do I know if you won't do that again?" he asked. "If you loved me, then you wouldn't want to be with nobody else."

"It goes both ways," she reminded him. "You keep hopping from woman to woman. If you loved me and wanted to be with just me, then you would."

"Those women don't mean nothing to me, April. You know I love you. Even though you broke my heart, I still love you," he said with feeling.

They hadn't resolved anything, but April let him spend the night. Now here it was six o'clock in the morning and she'd gotten used, once again.

Darren finished dressing and put on his shoes. He glared at her.

"See, that's the reason we can't be together. You have men calling all times of night. I can't trust you."

"I can't trust you either," she tossed back. "Every time I turn around you're with some bitch. Then you start acting like you don't have a son."

"I take care of my son. It's not like he want for nothing. That's just an excuse you use to keep doing what you're doing."

"Whatever! I don't have time to listen to this shit. Just get out."

Darren paused in the doorway. "Just remember. I tried to work things out. I ain't gonna try too many more times. I'm tired of being just your baby daddy!" He let the door slam on his way out which irritated the hell out of April.

"I don't need ya broke ass no way!" she yelled, mad because she'd lost precious hours of sleep messing around with his limp dick ass half the night. Now, she had to go to work tired, and she'd probably be late if she didn't get up right away.

She turned over and went back to sleep. An hour passed before Peaches woke her up.

"I missed the bus because I overslept," she said, not seeming to be upset about it at all.

April swore. If she wasn't going to be late before, she damn sure would be after driving Peaches to school. It was going to be one of those days.

Chapter Four

Brittany Anderson seethed with anger. She could physically strangle her husband with her bare hands. It was a good thing that he lived hundreds of miles away in another state.

She stopped at the bank to withdraw money and discovered that her checking account had a negative balance. She went inside thinking there had to be some simple mistake that could be easily corrected. Unfortunately, she only got worse news; her savings account had been wiped out too.

It seemed that her husband's past came back to haunt *her*. Creditors that he neglected to pay traced her accounts and garnished the funds. As long as a garnishment remained in force the bank could not close the accounts. The service representatives could only recommend that she cancel her direct deposit. This would prevent them from taking any further funds. However, that didn't do Brittany any good. Her rent was due and she had to pay childcare expenses for her two children. She needed her money, right then.

Brittany pulled into a parking space at Good Hands Insurance. She seriously considered backing out and leaving. She was in no mood to work. She felt sick to her stomach and had a headache.

She forced herself to get out of the car and go inside the building. She *had* to work. She needed to put in as much overtime as possible. Making ends meet would be tough with all of her money gone.

She mechanically went inside the building and made it to her desk. She plopped down at her workstation, still in shock.

She couldn't believe that all of *her* money disappeared because of Todd's mismanagement and frivolous spending.

"Selfish dog," she mumbled to herself. She couldn't wait to finalize their divorce. She couldn't stand his sorry ass.

She worked in the medical billings department processing insurance claims, which were abundant. The work was redundant, and the pay meager. At least she had a full-time job so she really couldn't complain.

She pulled herself together mentally, and got up to get work from a team leader. Their department allowed them to listen to music so she placed on her headphones. She busied herself with inputting claims, determined not dwell on her current financial situation. About fifteen minutes passed.

"Brittany?"

She looked up when she thought she heard her name being called.

"Did you call me?" she asked the girl standing next to her desk. She was pretty and appeared to be biracial or Hispanic.

"Do you drive a blue Honda?" the girl asked.

"Yes."

"Well, it looks like you got a flat," the girl told her.

"Are you serious?" Brittany exclaimed. How in the hell would she be able to get it fixed with no money? This was all she needed. She couldn't help herself; the tears began to flow.

She took off her headphones, got up and headed to the bathroom. She couldn't take any more bad news. She just couldn't. Now she had no choice but to call her mother and ask for help. She dreaded doing that. Brittany felt that her mother was the type who helped everyone except for her own family. She hated asking her for anything. She just didn't want to hear that woman's opinion. She'd also have to practically beg to illicit any help.

Teresa D. Patterson

Brittany stared in the mirror after washing her face. She looked a mess. Crying had made her eyes puffy and bloodshot.

The door opened and someone else entered the rest room. Brittany dried her face with a paper towel.

"You okay?" It happened to be the girl who had informed her of her flat tire.

"Yeah. Just one of those days," Brittany told her.

"If you need a ride home, let me know," the girl offered, heading for a stall.

"Okay. Er- what's your name?"

"April. April Dillard."

"Okay. Thanks. I'm going to go see if I can find Craig. Maybe he can change my tire. Bye."

"Bye." She heard from behind the door.

As soon as she left the bathroom she walked over to Craig's desk. Craig was an overly friendly guy who socialized with everyone. Being married didn't deter him from hitting on all the women who worked there. He wasn't the most handsome guy, but he was nice.

"What's up?" he greeted. His eyes lit up as soon as he saw her.

"Not much. I have a slight problem." Brittany told him about her flat tire. He said he'd help her change it on their break.

"So, ur- you free tonight?" he asked.

"Craig, I already told you, I'm married," she reminded him.

"Oh. Yeah, that's right. Well, tell your husband he's lucky." He laughed at his own joke. Brittany ignored him and walked away.

The things you have to put up with to get a little help, she thought. She was glad he agreed to change her tire, though.

Craig took off the flat and replaced it with the donut. Brittany made it to the daycare to pick up her children. She stopped by a shop on the north side of St. Petersburg to have her damaged tire repaired. They only charged five dollars to plug it. Thankfully, she could afford that.

After leaving the tire shop, she debated on whether or not to go to her mother's house, but decided against it. She'd just call her on the phone. Every time she stopped by, her mother would con her into doing something for her. Either it would be to put a permanent in her hair, do something with her computer or help with her real estate business. Brittany was not in the mood. The thought of going over there and being conned by her mother turned her off. She'd probably have her answer the phones, something that Brittany detested doing.

Brittany had just moved from an apartment complex into a house. She parked in the driveway noticing that the lawn needed to be mowed. A lot of work needed to be done on the house. It would just have to wait. The money in her savings had been for repairs. Now, she'd have to put those plans on the back burner.

She sent the kids to their room because she didn't feel like hearing any noise. Two boys could be rowdy and loud. She didn't need them running around while she prepared dinner. She had too much on her mind.

She prepared something easy for dinner. Macaroni and cheese and hotdogs would have to do. She was glad that her sons weren't picky eaters. While she fixed the food, her phone rang.

"Hello?"

"Hello?" her mother chirped.

Brittany let out a long breath. She had wanted to at least have time to relax before talking to her. Now, she had no choice.

Her mother talked for a while until she realized that Brittany wasn't participating in the conversation.

"What's wrong with you?" she asked.

"I want to kill your son-in-law," Brittany told her, flatly.

"Stop talking that silliness," her mother said.

"I'm not. If I had a gun and he was standing right here, I'd blow him away,"

"Why would you say something like that?" Brittany went on to explain what happened. Her mother listened, but didn't say much.

"I guess this means that you're going to need help," her mother finally said.

"I didn't say that- yet," Brittany replied.

"Well, I'll help you out of your bind, but I need for you to help me."

Brittany held her breath and waited for the bomb to drop. "You know I'm stressed out. It doesn't make any sense for you to have your real estate license and not help me out. So, I'll give you the money that you need, if you come help me out here." Brittany didn't really have a choice, did she?

"Alright, how soon do you need me?"

"I need you right now," her mom said with a laugh. Brittany didn't find it very amusing. "But, starting next week, you can come help me out after you get off work."

"Alright," she said without much enthusiasm.

Needless to say, she didn't feel like being bothered after she got off the phone with her mother. She cleaned up the kitchen then went to lie down. It was seven in the evening. She must have nodded off because the ringing phone awakened her.

"Hello?" It was Jarvis, a guy she'd met a few months earlier. Since they'd already hooked up a few times Jarvis called her whenever he got horny. She hadn't heard from him in a while though.

"Can I come over?" he asked, as though no time had transpired since she'd last seen him.

"No," she refused. Why did men always think they could pull that? They'd disappear then come back with no explanation, expecting to be able to pick up where they'd left off.

Out of the blue, Jarvis thought he could just make a booty call. She wasn't having it.

"What's wrong with you?"

"I had the worst day of my life. I don't feel good and I just want to sleep," she told him.

"Oh, well. I guess I caught you at a bad time. You sure you don't want me to stop by? I can make you feel better," he said in low tones.

"No, I don't want you to stop by," she reiterated. "Now, I'm going to sleep. Good night." She slammed the receiver down and pulled the plug.

Even though she'd hung up on Jarvis, he came over anyway. He continued to ring her doorbell until she finally opened the door. It didn't take much convincing on his part before they were in the bedroom.

Brittany let Jarvis have his way with her. Whatever he wanted to do, she agreed to it. He ended up handcuffing her wrists to her legs with two pair of handcuffs and working her over until she begged him to stop.

Jarvis hadn't ever met such a willing sexual participant. Brittany didn't mind getting as freaky as he wanted. That's why he kept coming back. She didn't ask for much except non-stop sex, which suited him fine. Hell, she usually ended up spending money on him if he asked her to. If he wanted to drink, she'd buy his favorite liquor. If he wanted to smoke some weed, she'd get that too. She'd even paid for some weekend type cruise that she wanted him to go on. He didn't have anything better to do, so he'd go. Besides, his lady, Tammy, would be at work that night. Since she worked from 11pm until 7am in the morning, he wouldn't have to explain anything.

He felt like a straight up pimp. He had two women and they were both clueless. Tammy, who was overweight and had self-esteem issues, worshipped the ground that he walked on. He had to be the best man she'd ever dated because she treated him like a king. She believed everything he told her, too. She never suspected him of being unfaithful.

Brittany assumed that he didn't have anyone, so he hadn't told her that he did. It wasn't his fault that she wanted to believe in fairytale romances. He would continue having the best of both worlds until one of them found out about the other.

He slapped Brittany on the ass, waking her up.

"Can I get a lil' slow smokin' head?" he asked. Where most women would have tripped, acting as if he'd disrespected them for asking for oral sex, Brittany didn't mind. She slid down in the bed and wrapped her succulent lips around his member. It immediately sprang to life. Damn, she had the best set of soup coolers and knew how to suck a dick off the bone.

He kept coming back because Tammy didn't know how to suck his dick correctly. She tried, but just used too much teeth. Brittany, on the other hand, could deep throat his shit the way he liked it. She licked and sucked it like it was the best tasting lollipop she'd ever had. She even took his balls in her mouth.

As Brittany hummed on his scrotum, he hoped that he never had to give up his sideline ho. He'd keep coming around as long as she didn't trip. Once she started acted like she owned him, he would be out of there.

Chapter Five

*H*appiness rushed over Camille when the temp agency called and offered her a job. She'd be working at an insurance agency, doing data entry beginning the following Monday. She knew Dexter wasn't too pleased about her working, but he'd just have to deal with it. She didn't want to be one of those sit-at-home wives, who let their husbands handle everything. If she became totally dependant on Dexter, what would she do if he ever decided to up and leave?

Dexter told her he wouldn't accept any money from her paycheck. He said it would be strictly for her personal use, to do with as she pleased. She already had it spent on stuff for the baby. She couldn't wait to find out the sex of the child.

Since she wasn't experiencing morning sickness anymore, she was pleasant to be around again. Dexter came home on time every day and they made love every night. The two of them behaved like a newlywed couple should behave. They didn't have one single argument all week.

Camille wanted to spice up their love life, so she began trying new things. She went on-line to Black Expressions.com and ordered a variety of books. One entitled A 101 Ways to Please Your Man caught her interest so she purchased it. She also bought one called Erotic Massage. Both books gave her all kinds of nice-nasty ideas on making love to Dexter.

That night, she placed candles all around the bathroom. She ran a bubble bath and was soaking in the warm water when Dexter came home. He found her in the tub, sipping on non-alcoholic champagne and eating chocolates.

"Hey, baby," he greeted, his eyes shining.

"Hey, sweetheart," she responded. "How was your day?"

"You know, just like the saying goes, "Another day, another dollar," he replied.

"Well, come on and join me. Come relax." She reached over and grabbed the Moet that she'd bought just for him and poured some of it into a wine glass.

Dexter smiled as he unbuttoned his shirt. Camille had surprised him all week. Monday, she had strawberries and whip cream. Lord, he never imagined all the many ways you could use that stuff. Tuesday, it had been velvet bed sheets and pillowcases, complete with the rose petals. Once again, she had shown him how to use fruit. Before the night was over she became a banana split. He didn't know if she'd ever be able to get all of the chocolate syrup out of those sheets. Wednesday, it had been the Pineapple Trick. Camille took some sliced Dole pineapples in the can and froze them. Then, she used them to bring him great satisfaction. He got his daily allowance of fruit as well as satisfaction. Now, here it was, Thursday, and Camille had all of this waiting for him. He could become very spoiled.

Dexter stripped naked and stood before her. She could see his arousal and that pleased her. She'd take care of that really soon.

Dexter slid into the tub of bubbles. Their bodies touched as he got behind her. She could feel his erection pressed against her back. She handed him his drink.

Dexter took a moment to savor the Moet then placed the champagne glass down. He reached for Camille, caressing her soapy body. He ran the suds over her back, shoulders and then her breasts. She moaned aloud.

"You're not tired of making love?" he whispered in her ear.

"No. I want you every night. Maybe it's the hormonal changes brought on because of the baby."

Dexter gently caressed her stomach. "I can't wait to thank you, Junior," he said to her belly. She laughed, leaning back into his embrace.

"How do you know that it's not a girl?" she said.

"It doesn't matter. I just want a healthy child. Either way, I'll love him or her with all of my heart."

"Me too," she said quietly. "I'm so glad that I met you, Dexter. I'm proud to be carrying your child. I'm going to be the best mother."

"I know you will, because you're the best wife," he told her.

Dexter couldn't stop the guilt that ate at his heart. Camille was the best, but that hadn't stopped him from having lunch with Meredith again that afternoon. Meredith demanded more of his time each day and he hadn't found the strength to resist her yet.

From day one, he told her about his marital status. She said she respected his honesty. Nonetheless, the chemistry between them could not be denied. Even though Camille had been nothing but perfect lately, he still felt attracted to Meredith.

Dexter's thoughts drifted…

Meredith Walker had come on as his new secretary. He had left hiring new employees to his assistant, Bill. He hadn't expected his secretary to be so beautiful. Once he saw her, he questioned Bill about his decision to hire her.

Bill, a middle-aged man with a bald spot and graying hair, seemed puzzled that Dexter would even ask.

"You said to hire the most experienced person for the job. Well, she knows the construction business like the back of my hand. She's done this type of work for over five years. She even has a college degree," he informed Dexter.

"I'm sure you made the right decision, Bill. Well, I guess I'd better go inside and introduce myself, formally."

He'd only seen Meredith in passing. She'd been working for him for three days by then. He convinced himself that he'd postponed the meeting because of a very busy week. He and his crew arrived at 5:30 am and worked until 6:00 pm or 7:00 pm in the evening. By the time they arrived back at the office, Meredith had left for the day.

Dexter gave Bill some instructions concerning a construction site and headed into the building.

Meredith was making coffee when he entered.

"Good morning, Mrs. Walker," he greeted. She turned when she heard his voice.

"Good morning!" Meredith smiled and he noticed that she had even, white teeth. "It's a pleasure to finally meet you," she exclaimed, turning away from the coffeepot and walking towards him with her hand extended. Well, she was certainly friendly.

"Hello, I'm Dexter Gray," he said.

"Meredith Walker." They shook hands. Dexter felt a slight tingle at the touch of their fingers.

"I just wanted to take this opportunity to welcome you aboard."

"Thank you," she smiled again. Meredith was tall, around five ten, nice figure, slender waistline. She resembled Vanessa Williams-Fox, the singer/actress. She even had the same color hazel eyes.

"Well, it's a pleasure to meet you. I'll get with you later to discuss a few job duties. I'm sure Bill is doing a great job showing you the ropes."

"Actually, he's doing a wonderful job," she said with delight. "But I do have a few questions and concerns. Maybe we can get together for lunch?" she suggested.

Dexter tried to think of an excuse off the top of his head, to back down, but he couldn't. Instead, he found himself agreeing to take her to lunch that evening. That's how it had all began. Innocent enough...

Dexter hadn't realized that his thoughts had drifted so far. It finally registered in his mind that the water in the tub had grown cold. He nudged Camille, who had nodded off.

"Baby, let's go to bed," he said quietly.

"Sure."

They got out of the tub and wrapped up in big, fluffy towels. Dexter helped Camille dry her back. He wanted to stop thinking about Meredith. He wanted to get her face out of his mind. Camille was his wife and that's the way it would stay.

That night, Dexter would make love to Camille slowly and passionately. He wanted to give her as much pleasure as she'd given him all week.

He stood at the end of the bed and gazed at her nakedness as she lay in the center of the sheets. He reached down and brought her foot up to his mouth. He began to suck her toes. He sucked each one, individually. Then, he placed all five

toes in his mouth at once. It was the most exquisite act that
Camille had ever experienced. Next, he did the other foot. He
kissed her from head to toe, leaving no part of her untouched
by his wet lips and sleek tongue. Soon, he knelt at the center
of her. She was hot and ready. He smelled her feminine scent
and it aroused him further. He tasted her sweetness and made
her moan and scream his name aloud. He didn't stop. He had
her grabbing the sides of his head, trying to pull him into her.
She screamed as she shivered and reached climax.

"So, you like that, huh?" he asked. He already knew her
answer by the satisfied look on her face.

"You've never done that to me before," she told him,
moving into his embrace.

"I didn't want to scare you. I don't know what you can
handle since you're so new at this sex thing."

"Dexter, I'm not a virgin anymore. You're supposed to
teach me everything that pleases you. Besides, I did watch a
few tapes," she confessed.

"Tapes? What kind of types?" he wanted to know.

"You know, those Rated-X kind," she told him and Dexter
chuckled.

He found that hard to believe. Not his shy, little Camille?
Watching pornography?

"What were the titles?" he asked, curiously.

"One was called *My Baby Got Back- Too*. And let me see,
the other one was *Bootylicious, Raise the Roof* or something
to that effect."

Dexter cracked up when she explained what happened on
the tapes. The porn flicks actually turned her off. She said
she'd rather make her own tape than to sit through that.

"So, will you be home on time tomorrow?" she asked,
stroking his chest fondly as she lay sideways.

"I'm not sure. I'll try," he told her, immediately noticing the disappointed look on her face. "But, if I'm running late, I'll call you. I promise," he added quickly.

"Okay. Everything has been so perfect this week," she said. "I wish that things could stay like this forever." She yawned and snuggled closer to him. Soon, he could hear her gentle breathing as she slept.

Forever is a long time, Dexter thought. Usually when things went well for a period of time, it never failed for something to come along and mess it up. That something happened to be Meredith.

Dexter remembered the conversation that took place between him and Meredith at lunch earlier that day.

Meredith immediately made her attraction to him known. She didn't try to hide it. She even went so far as to tell him outright.

"I know that you're married, but we can be very discreet. I'd never tell a soul if you decide to begin an affair," she said sweetly.

"Meredith, I'm not that type of man. Besides, it would be unfair to you. Would you be content to just be someone's mistress? Don't you think better of yourself than that?"

"Of course I do. It's just that I'm the type of woman that knows what she wants and I go after it." She stared at him intently. "I want you."

"I'm already taken," he insisted.

"Then why are you here with me?" she asked brazenly. "If you're happy and content in your marriage, shouldn't you be having lunch with her?"

"My wife is pregnant. She hasn't been feeling up to it. Besides, my personal life is none of your business." Dexter didn't mean to sound harsh, but he had to lay his cards on the table. He could see that Meredith might turn out to be a difficult person to get rid of if he did get involved with her. He had to put a stop to it now. "Meredith, you're a very beautiful woman. If things were different, if I'd met you at a different time, maybe we could have had something. But, the fact is, I'm married. Point blank. I do not want to begin an affair. After today, I'm afraid I won't be having any more meetings with you. I don't want to do anything to jeopardize my marriage."

Meredith sat back in her chair and regarded him.

"So, you're telling me no?" she asked. "Is that what you're saying, Dexter?" Obviously, she didn't believe him.

"If that's the way you're taking it," he replied.

"Is that your final decision?" She smiled, reached across the table and grasped his hand. Dexter snatched away quickly, as if burned.

"Yes, Meredith. What part of "no" don't you understand?" He felt irritated. Who was Meredith Walker, anyway? Just because she was supermodel beautiful, didn't give her a right to just stake her claim on anyone she wanted.

Dexter had to admit that it flattered him. What man wouldn't be? He had even flirted back. Hell, it wasn't every day that an attractive woman came on to him, but he would not encourage it any further. From that day forward it would be strictly business-related. Meredith would just have to accept it.

"Well, I'll suggest you reconsider your decision," Meredith told him. "It will be between two consenting adults. We'll be very discreet. Your wife will not have to know a thing about us."

"Meredith, you're talking crazy," he said. "Now, finish your lunch."

Meredith complied, reluctantly. She could tell his resistance to her had weakened. His marriage must not be built on a strong foundation since she could shake it. She sensed it from the way Dexter avoided her gaze.

"Meredith, I'm not trying to hurt your feelings or anything," he stated after a brief silence. "I just want to maintain a strictly, professional, working relationship. That's the way it has to be," he told her.

"That's fine," she replied. "I'll accept that decision." *"For now,"* she added to herself, taking a sip from her drink. She eyed his broad shoulders and muscular arms. She wondered what it would feel like to have them wrapped around her. If luck was on her side, she'd find out.

Dexter turned over on his back, sat up and pulled the comforter over his wife. Looking at the digital clock on the nightstand, he saw that it was still early, nine-thirty. He got up and went into the living room to watch television. On B.E.T. they were running a reality series about the female rapper, Lil' Kim. They were counting down the days until she'd serve time in prison. Dexter became engrossed in it. Once a commercial aired, he headed to the kitchen. He couldn't believe he still had an appetite after such a large dinner. It had to have been brought on by the workout he'd given Camille.

He began fixing a turkey sandwich. He placed all of the necessary items on the counter. The phone chose that moment to ring. He put down the spoon of Miracle Whip and lifted the cordless off the receiver.

"Hello?"

"Dexter? This is Meredith. I'm sorry to call so late, but I locked my keys in my car by accident. I was hoping that you could pick me up and take me home to get the spare?"

"Well, okay. Where are you?"

"I'm so sorry for disturbing you. I just didn't know anyone else to call," she said. She told him her location, which he wrote down on the adhesive note pad affixed to the refrigerator.

"I'll be there in a few minutes," he said and hung up the phone.

Dexter went back into the bedroom and pulled on a pair of Nike shorts and a tee shirt. Camille was still sleeping soundly as he got his keys off the dresser and headed out.

About fifteen minutes later he pulled his Navigator next to Meredith's Lexus. She stood on the sidewalk in front of a beauty salon, talking on her cell phone. She ended her conversation when she saw him.

"Hey, glad you made it," she called to him. He got out, walked around the vehicle and opened the passenger's door for her.

"So, where to?" he asked, climbing back behind the wheel.

"Pinellas Point Drive," she told him.

"Okay, I know where that is. How did you manage to lock your keys in the car?" he asked, making small talk.

"I went inside to check on things. That's my salon, by the way," she added.

"Oh really?" he didn't know what else to say, so he left it at that.

"I guess I just forgot to take my keys out of the ignition."

"Well, it happens." He turned on the radio. Some hip-hop station played a song by Missy Elliot. Meredith reached over and changed the dial.

"All of that rapping and fast music gives me a headache," she explained, putting it on 98.7 FM, a jazz station. Dexter liked the other song, but he said nothing.

They drove in silence. Dexter kept replaying the conversation they'd had earlier in his mind. It wasn't long before he pulled into the driveway in front of Meredith's house. From what he could see in the dark, it was beautiful. Pinellas Point Drive was located in the ritzy section of town. He was considering purchasing a home on "the Point," but he hadn't decided yet.

"I'll be right back," she said. She got out and went up the steps. Dexter took that opportunity to change the dial back to his station. If he wanted to listen to jazz he would have put it on jazz. Women.

Within minutes, Meredith returned with her spare key.

"You don't have to take me back to my car right away," she told him. "You could come inside and have a drink."

"No. I can't do that," he declined.

"Why not Dexter? Afraid of what might happen?" she asked, smirking.

"Nothing will happen, Meredith. We've been through this before. Will you just stop?" It dawned on him that the key locked in the car might have been a ploy to get him out to her house.

Meredith turned to him and placed her hand on his knee.

"Why are you playing hard to get?" she asked.

"I'm not playing. Meredith, I don't have time for your games." He pushed her hand off his knee. "I'm taking you back to your car. In the future, if something like this happens, you need to call somebody else, like AAA Auto Club."

Dexter returned home a little before ten thirty. He went into the kitchen to finish making his sandwich. He couldn't believe he'd spent almost an hour with Meredith. He had been too glad to drop her off and get as far away from her as he could.

When he saw Camille sitting at the table it startled him. He expected her to still be in bed.

She stared at him with distrustful eyes.

"Where have you been?" she asked tightly.

"I went to help someone who locked their keys in the car."

"Well, you sure rushed off in a hurry. You couldn't even finish fixing your damn sandwich. That slut must be important to you," she snapped.

"Camille, what are you talking about? If something's on your mind, just say it."

"Who is Meredith Walker?" She glared at him expecting another lie. "That *is* who you went to see, right?"

Dexter sighed. "Camille, it's not what you think."

"I checked the caller ID. So, I know it was a woman who called here."

"I never said it wasn't," he began. "I did go to-"

"I called the number," she interrupted.

"But-"

"She answered her cell phone and told me that you were getting ready to head to her house."

"If you'll just let me explain-" he started.

"You don't have to explain shit to me!" she yelled. "You were with someone else. How could you, Dexter? How can you leave my bed and go hop into someone else's?" she asked, accusingly.

"Camille, shut up and listen to me," he told her, finally losing his temper. He was tired of being accused of something that he hadn't done. He had let it go on for long enough. It seemed to bother Camille when he never responded to her tantrums. Tonight, he wasn't having it. "Nothing like that happened," he continued. "I only took her to get her spare key. That's all. Now, I don't know what you think went on. But whatever you're thinking right now, you are wrong."

"Why should I believe you?" she asked, beginning to cry.

"Because I'm your husband," he yelled, not caving in because of her tears. Her accusations really bothered him. It almost made him want to take Meredith up on her offer. It wasn't like she wasn't willing.

"Well, who is she, Dexter? Who the hell is Meredith Walker, anyway?"

"She's my new secretary," he admitted.

"Oh, so you have a new secretary?" she asked sarcastically. "You never told me."

"Why should I, Camille? I don't feel the need to explain every business decision that I make with you. You're my wife, not my damn boss." He stalked out of the room, forgetting all about the sandwich. He'd lost his appetite anyway.

He left her sitting at the table crying. He felt annoyance more than anything. For the past two weeks he had to admit, he felt tempted to stray from his marriage. But, he hadn't. When Camille blew up at him for little or no reason it made him furious.

He knew that it looked bad. Plus, the confusion he felt inside didn't help matters any. His attraction to Meredith didn't make him guilty. He hadn't acted on his feelings. He hadn't overstepped any boundaries. He would stick to his marriage vows, no matter how difficult Camille became. He contributed all of her mood swings to her pregnancy. Hopefully, it would all pass soon.

Dexter went to grab his pillow. He didn't care whether or not he was in the doghouse. He wouldn't give Camille the satisfaction of kicking him out of their bed again. He got a blanket out of the linen closet and made up the couch to sleep on.

Camille sat at the table for a while longer. Her tears had turned into sniffles. She knew that she'd probably overreacted again. She just hadn't known what to think when she woke up and found Dexter gone. She had waited for him, thinking that maybe he went to the store for bread or something. When the minutes turned into an hour, she picked up the phone. That's when she saw the unfamiliar number on the caller ID, which prompted her to dial it.

Camille got up from the table and went into the bathroom to wash her face. She had a throbbing headache and felt sick to her stomach. She needed to calm down. Stress wasn't good for her or the baby.

When she walked into the bedroom she noticed that Dexter had taken his pillow. That only increased her suspicions and brought her anger back full force. If he wasn't guilty, why was he sleeping on the couch?

Her made was made up. She would personally introduce herself to Meredith Walker. She wasn't going to give up her husband without a fight. She wanted to see exactly what the bitch had that she didn't.

Chapter Six

April sat in the break room of the Good Hands Insurance Company. She'd gone to a fast food restaurant located nearby to get a chicken sandwich, fries and a soft drink. She chewed quickly because she only had ten minutes left before her lunch break ended. She kept telling herself to bring a lunch so she wouldn't have to leave to get something. Even though there were places close to them, it took at least fifteen minutes to drive there and get back. That barely gave her enough time to wolf down her food.

Brittany entered carrying a Slim Fast shake. She saw April and smiled brightly. "Hi April. How are you?" she greeted and came to sit down at the table in a seat across from her.

"Hello," April replied. "I'm alright." She wondered if Brittany really cared. She didn't trust most women and didn't really allow herself to open up to many. Brittany seemed sincere enough, but you could never tell. She remembered Brittany's flat tire.

"Hey, did you get your car taken care of?" she asked.

"Yeah, I got it fixed. But I still had to end up borrowing money from my mom. I had to buy a new tire, anyway. A few days later, one of my other tires blew out." She shook the Slim Fast and popped it open. "This week has been so stressful. I'm going out tonight. I need to get drunk."

"I know that's right," April laughed. She could relate. Brittany was looking better by the minute since she'd mentioned going out. "So, where you going?"

"I might go to Club Atlanta. They have happy hour on Friday nights. Then again, I haven't been to the new club yet. I might check it out."

"What club is that?"

"Club XS."

"Oh, I heard about that club. The radio station broadcasts there live, doing the Friday Night Bomb. I want to check that out," April told her.

"Hey, we can go together, if you want," Brittany suggested.

"Alright. Let me give you my number." April wrote down her number and slid it to Brittany. Having someone to hang out with when she hit the clubs was right up her alley.

Brittany really opened up and began telling her the story of Jarvis. Jarvis had lied and told her that he didn't have a girlfriend, but she'd found out otherwise. The girl had called her house because Jarvis, stupidly, called her from his girlfriend's phone. During the conversation, Brittany found out that they had dated for three years and had even gotten engaged at one point in time.

"Men are such dogs," she finished.

"I hope you stopped seeing him," April said.

"Not yet. I just want to teach his girlfriend a lesson. She had no business calling my house. It's not my fault that her man can't be faithful."

"Well, you need to be careful. Women these days are dangerous. I'd just cut him loose and find somebody else," April advised.

"I will, but I still have to get back at him, first." She felt livid because she'd taken Jarvis on a weekend cruise. Had she known that he had a girlfriend, she wouldn't have wasted her money. She deserved to get something back for all her wasted efforts.

"Well, I have to get back in there. My break is over," April said. She began wrapping her half-eaten sandwich up to save for later.

"Mine is too, but I don't care. They don't know when we left because we don't have to punch in or out."

"Well that's true," April agreed.

"Take ten more minutes and finish your lunch. You paid for it, so eat it."

April was beginning to like Brittany more and more. She usually played by the rules on jobs that she liked. But, she really didn't care too much for processing claims. Ten extra minutes wouldn't hurt anything. She picked up her sandwich and smiled at Brittany in conspiracy.

Brittany knocked on the door to April's apartment. She answered, wearing a short, pink dress that tied behind the neck. It was that glossy kind of material. Of course, she had on her heels. She had flat ironed her thick hair and it now hung straight. "Come on in. I got some Mud Slide in the blender. You want some?"

"Sure. It's not too strong, is it?" Brittany asked. "I don't drink that often. So when I do, it goes straight to my head. I want to be able to drive."

Brittany wore a tight, electric blue bodysuit. It was shiny and clung to her figure. She also wore heels.

"You'll be alright. This isn't strong at all. It tastes like a chocolate milk shake to me." April poured their drinks into plastic cups. "I don't have any straws," she said, handing Brittany a cup.

"I might have some in my glove department. We better get going if we want to get there before the crowd," Brittany told her.

"Do a lot of people be there?" April asked.

"Yeah, the line is usually down the street, depending on what time you arrive. If we get there before eleven, we won't have to pay."

"Good, I can save my lil' ten dollars for drinks," April said. They headed out.

In the car, Brittany checked the glove compartment and located the straws. She handed one to April. "We're going to be sippin' on some sy~rup," she sang and blasted the stereo.

They both slurped their drinks as they listened to some booty-shaking music. Hyped up for Friday night, they made it to Ybor City before eleven o'clock. By the time they got to Club XS, the club was charging admissions. Brittany hadn't exaggerated; the line was extra long, curled nearly around the building.

As soon as they got inside, Brittany and April headed straight for the bar to order drinks. Since she only had $4 left, April ordered a Heineken. Brittany got a Sprite. They sat at the bar for a while, sipping on their drinks.

It wasn't long before a tall, medium built guy approached Brittany. She checked him out and decided that he passed inspection. He was kind of cute.

"Want to dance?" he asked and she agreed.

"Come on," she told April, not wanting to leave her at the bar alone. April followed them to the dance floor, feeling like a third wheel.

Brittany and the guy seemed to hit it off. They tried to talk over the loud music, which was nearly impossible. A slim guy with dreads began dancing behind April. When the song ended, he offered to buy her a drink.

"Hey, I'm going to get another drink," she hollered to Brittany, hoping that she heard. She followed the guy off the floor.

"My name is Jerrod," he said with an accent of some kind. "What be your name, gul?"

April tried not to laugh. "April," she said. "Where you from?" she asked.

"My native land is Jamaica. But, I jus' move down here from Baltimore," he told her. He raised his arm in the air and tried to get the bartender's attention. He was unsuccessful. "Damn it, mon!"

It took a few minutes, but he finally succeeded in getting the bartender. He bought her a Hennessy and Coke and a shot of Courvoisier cognac for himself.

April sipped her drink. She didn't want to appear ungrateful, but she really wasn't interested in the Jamaican. She just didn't like his hair, never having been too fond of dreads.

She kept him company until he ordered another drink. While his back was turned, she quickly slipped away.

She searched for Brittany but saw no signs of her amidst the crowd. Guys tried to hit on her as she walked around. She finished her drink and headed for the bathroom. Some forceful idiot grabbed her by the arm.

"What the fuck you doing here?" It was Darren.

"The same thing you doing here? Let go of my arm," she told him.

"I better not see you dancing with no one in here," he told her.

"Man, you are tripping. You don't tell me what to do."
She snatched her arm away.

"I'm not playing, April. Don't get nobody fucked up
tonight," he threatened.

April could not believe how he was behaving. Darren had
never acted so jealous before. What was wrong with him?
Then, she caught a whiff of his breath.

"Whoa. You're drunk,' she said and backed away.

"I ain't drunk," he slurred. "I ain't drunk. You just try me
and you'll see what a drunk nigga will do." He staggered off
into the crowd.

April continued on into the bathroom and waited about
five minutes before one became available. She breathed a
sigh of relief when she finally got her chance.

The floor inside the stall was littered with used toilet
paper. The sanitary napkin disposal was full and over-
flowing, and the toilet wasn't flushed. It appeared to be
clogged, but April couldn't hold her pee any longer.

She refused to sit down but squatted over the seat to
relieve her bowels. Her legs almost gave out because it took
so long. She finally finished, managing not to pee on the floor
or herself. Of course, there wasn't any toilet paper. Lucky for
her, she had some napkins in her purse. It wasn't Charmin,
but it would have to do.

When she came out the bathroom stall, she saw Brittany at
the mirror refreshing her lipstick.

"Girl, I was looking for you. I just ran into Darren." She
headed to the sink to wash her hands, telling Brittany about
what happened.

"You think he's going to start something?" Brittany asked,
surveying her hair in the mirror.

"I don't know. But, I'm not leaving. We just got here. If he got a problem with me being in the same club, then he can leave."

"Who dat is? That's just yo' baby daddy." Brittany laughed, singing the rap song by T Byrd. "That's just yo' baby daddy."

April's night went from bad to worse. Darren kept his word and showed his ass. He interrupted April from dancing with a fine guy who she was faintly interested in getting to know better. Darren pushed the guy, which caused him to spill his drink all over the dance floor. April had been so embarrassed when he wouldn't let anyone dance with her the rest of the night. He stood guarding her like a protective watchdog.

"I can't believe that asshole clowned like that," she told Brittany on their way to the car.

"It's love. Love makes men act irrationally."

"Fuck that shit. His ass was just drunk." She got into the car and turned on her cell phone. She had eight messages. When she listened, all of them were from Darren.

"I'm going to hook up with the guy I met tonight," Brittany told her.

"Which one? The tall guy that you danced with earlier?"

"Yeah."

"Y'all hooking up already?" April asked.

"Yeah. He's coming over at 4:00."

April didn't say a word. She wasn't the one to judge. After all, it was none of her business. She hoped that Brittany would be smart and use precautions. You never knew about picking up strange men in the club. You could get yourself a real nutcase, and you could catch something that you may not be able to get rid of.

"Well, Darren left me eight messages. I bet he's gonna be at my apartment when I get there."

"That's what you get for putting it on him. He can't let you go." They laughed as Brittany pulled out of the parking garage. All in all, it had been a good night until Darren had shown up.

Chapter Seven

Brittany had a date with Craig. The night that she'd met him at the club, he came over, but they ended up talking until they both fell asleep. It was going on three weeks and Craig hadn't pressured her about having sex. She had broken her record. She usually gave some up by the second date, if not the first. Since Craig hadn't tried to jump into bed with her right away, this convinced her he was different. He really cared about her. She had finally met a man that she could trust.

Craig lived in Brandon. Since that was a forty-five minute drive from where she stayed, he'd spend the weekend with her. He'd usually come over on Friday night. They'd hook up and do something on Saturday then he'd leave on Sunday. It became a routine.

Brittany fell hard for Craig. She even thought about marriage, for the second time. Her kids were already crazy about him. He had even met her mother, and she hadn't turned her nose up at him like she usually did when Brittany introduced her to someone. Her mother was stuck on her soon-to-be ex-husband. No one could take his place, as far as she was concerned. So, it surprised Brittany that her mother actually took to Craig.

Craig fit the criteria of a decent guy. He worked full time. He was also in the Army Reserves. He hung out with his friends from time to time, but didn't do a lot of excessive club hopping. At least, that's the story he told.

He swore to Brittany that he didn't have anyone special in his life. He also said that he didn't have any children. She prided herself in having found a true winner. Not many twenty-four year old, Black men came without some sort of excess baggage. She was almost certain that there were no bones in Craig's closet.

Even though they hadn't had sex, it was leading up to it. Brittany could feel the sexual tension building inside her. But, she'd be willing to wait as long as Craig felt they needed to.

"I don't think it will be right until you get your divorce," he told her one night. They were going into their second week together.

They'd gone out and Brittany consumed a little more alcohol than she was accustomed to. She got horny and wanted to consummate their relationship. However, Craig, who could control his liquor, pointed out some things to her. He pushed her away, gently.

"We can't do this, Brittany. I'm an honorable man. I don't want to feel like I've taken advantage of someone's wife or committed adultery."

Brittany felt so special. She called an attorney the next day to schedule an appointment. As soon as she could complete the necessary paperwork, she'd be on her way to being free. She couldn't wait to start the divorce proceedings. She wanted to speed things up. As soon as she ridded herself of Todd, she could place Craig's engagement ring on her finger.

Brittany floated on cloud nine. She was in love. Saturday rolled around and they were going to dinner, then out to the movies. Craig hadn't made it on Friday, as usual, because he'd taken his grandmother to the hospital. She had sprained her ankle.

Brittany got her little sister to baby sit the children and waited for Craig to show up. He called her around five to confirm their plans.

Brittany started to worry when it approached nine and he hadn't arrived. She called his grandmother's house. Craig didn't have a pager or a cell phone. He thought they were a waste of money.

"Hello?"

"Hello, Mrs. Rivers? This is Brittany. Is Craig there?"

"No, baby. I haven't seen or heard from him all week," she informed. This puzzled Brittany. Craig had told her that he lived with his grandmother. He said he stayed there to help look after her because she didn't like to be in the house by herself.

"Well, how are you feeling? Is your ankle better?" she thought to ask.

"My ankle is just fine. Why wouldn't it be, honey?"

"Didn't you have to go to the emergency room last night?" Brittany's heartbeat quickened. She prayed that Mrs. Rivers gave her the answer that she sought.

"No, baby. I'm doing jus' fine. I didn't go anywhere last night. Jus' watched me some Jeopardy. I like that show."

"Oh, okay. I must have misunderstood Craig. Well, thank you, Mrs. Rivers."

"You're welcome, sugar. Good-bye."

"Bye." Brittany slammed the phone down. "That lying son-of-a-bitch," she swore aloud. Where the hell was he? When and if he did show up, she would give him a piece of her mind. No way would another man walk all over her again. She was tired of all the games. If Craig couldn't come up with an explanation that suited her, somebody would get hurt.

Brittany paced the floor for another half an hour. Craig never showed up and he never bothered to call. Finally, she gave up. She took her sister home and returned to consume half a bottle of Arbor Mist. Then, she went to bed semi-drunk and fuming inside. Every dog had its day, and the next day, Craig's flea-ridden ass would have his.

Of course Craig called on Sunday full of apologies. He told her that his car broke down on the way and he had to hitch a ride back to Brandon. Then, he got his brother to come back with him and they managed to fix the car. Once they fixed the problem, it was late and he didn't want to disturb her. So, that was the reason he hadn't called.

"Well, what about your grandmother's ankle?" Brittany questioned. "I called there for you and she said that her ankle was fine. She never went to the emergency room." Brittany was certain that she had caught him in a lie, but Craig had an excuse ready.

"That's not the grandmother that had to go to the ER. It was my other grandma- my father's mama. Brittany, why do you think I'd lie to you? I told you, we got something good and I don't want to mess it up. I'm doing everything I can to prove that I care about you. I'll be over there today if you want to see me. You can make dinner."

"Well, I don't have anything to cook. I'm out of groceries," she told him, still not quite ready to give in.

"That's no problem. We'll go to the store and get whatever you need. I'll see you in about an hour."

"Craig?"

"Yeah?"

"You need a pager or a cell phone. Let's look into getting you one," she told him.

"Er, um. Well, we'll discuss that when I get there. Okay?"

"Okay. Bye."

True to his word he showed up an hour later. Brittany wanted to stay angry with him, but she couldn't find a real reason to be mad. She believed that he had car problems.

After all, he did drive an older model car, what they call a "Hoopty." It surprised her that the piece of junk was still on the road. He should have retired it to the junkyard years before.

When he took her in his arms and kissed her passionately, the rest of her resolve melted away. So what if they hadn't hooked up the night before. Craig was there now and that was all that mattered.

They went to Sam's Club, a store where you could buy food in bulk. Craig told her that she could get anything that she wanted. She tried not to show out, but hell, she figured she might never get another opportunity. So, she went down one aisle and up another. By the time they checked out, there was over $350.00 worth of groceries. Once they left that store, he suggested they make a stop at the meat market. Brittany didn't mind at all. He offered to pay for everything and she didn't protest.

Brittany had never had a man buy her groceries or much of anything, to be completely honest. She usually did most of the spending, subconsciously trying to buy their affection. With that simple act of kindness, Craig completely won her over.

Craig behaved like the perfect boyfriend that weekend. He paid attention to her and showered her with his generosity. Instead of having Brittany cook that evening, he took her out to dinner. Then, they went to see the theater, to see *The Matrix*. After the movie ended, they walked on the beach and watched the stars. Brittany felt just like one of those stars- in heaven.

Back at the house, Craig gave her a full body massage with hot oil. At first, she relaxed and lay there, letting him knead her tired muscles. Soon, it began to feel erotic. Brittany wanted him more than ever, but Craig continued to hold back. However, he didn't object to her pleasuring him with her lips. She had no objections when he did the same to her. But, she wanted to feel him inside of her. He had to be the most patient man she'd ever met. It drove her crazy.

Sunday morning Brittany got up early. Craig had to leave, so she wanted to make the day special by surprising him with breakfast in bed.

When she sat the eggs and milk on the table, she accidentally knocked his wallet on the floor. She went to pick it up and several things fell out. Her eye caught the name on the Social Security card that lay on the floor. Craig Thomas Booker Jr. Craig wasn't a junior.

Or was he? There was also another Social Security card with the name Jasmine Tremaine Booker. Why did he have children's social security cards in his possession? Could they possibly be his kids?

Brittany didn't want to jump to conclusions. She would calmly ask him about it over breakfast. She was determined not to accuse him. Things were going so well and she didn't want to mess up the flow.

Craig seemed genuinely pleased with breakfast. Brittany waited until he'd finished eating to bring up the subject of kids.

"Craig, I know I've asked you this before, but do you have any children?" she said, as she took the tray with the remaining traces of his breakfast left on it.

"I told you that I don't." He sat on the edge of the bed and rubbed his stomach.

"Then who is Craig Thomas Booker Jr. and Jasmine Tremaine Booker?"

At first a guilty expression crossed his face, but he hid it quickly. Then, he gave her an irritated smirk.

"Why have you been going through my personal stuff? What is it? You don't trust me?"

"That's not it at all. Your wallet fell on the floor and some of your stuff fell out. It's not like I went searching for incriminating information. Besides, that is not the point. Explain Craig Thomas Booker Jr. and Jasmine Tremaine," she insisted.

"Why are you always looking for the worse to happen, Brittany? It's like you want me to be lying to you. You want me to be untrustworthy. It's like I'm guilty until proven innocent," he said, turning to look at her with a puppy-dog expression on his face.

"That speech is all well and good, but that doesn't explain why you'd tell me you don't have children, when you do."

"I don't have any kids," he said in a defensive tone.

"Then why do you have their social security cards in you wallet?"

"Those are my sister's kids. She said that I could claim them on my income tax if I give her some money. She let me hold their social security cards because I have to go to H & R Block next week."

Brittany didn't buy it. "Why would your sister name her son after you? That doesn't even make sense to me."

"She didn't name him after me. Her son's father is named Craig Thomas Booker, too. I know it sounds like a lie. But it's not. You can call her and ask her if you don't believe me."

"Whatever. Craig, I don't have time for this. If you have children, you have children. You don't have to lie. Do you think that it would make a difference to me? I can't hold that against you. I have children myself." She stared at him, waiting for him to break down and be honest. He didn't come clean.

"Well, it's different for you. You were married when you had your children," he said.

"So, are you telling me that you have kids?" she pressed.

"No, I'm not saying that. I do not have any kids, Brittany."

"So, that's you story and you're sticking with it?" She stared at him hard.

"Yes. I don't have any kids," he said.

"Okay. Don't let it come up later on down the line that you do have children. Now is the perfect opportunity for you to tell me. I'm giving you a chance to be honest. If I find out that you do have kids, and that you lied to me about something so important, I will no longer be as understanding about it. I'm just telling you now."

"You ain't got nothing to worry about. I'm not hiding anything from you. Stop being so filled with distrust." He reached for her hand and pulled her towards him. At first she resisted, but soon she weakened and sat on his lap. He kissed her deeply. "Thank you for breakfast," he told her. "You're a very special lady. I've never met anyone like you. You know how to take care of a man." He began kissing her down her neck and caressing her thighs. "Let me take care of you right now," he said suggestively.

"But, I thought we were going to wait," she protested, halfheartedly.

"I know, baby. But, I need you. I can't wait any longer." He pulled her down on the bed beside him and stared into her eyes. "Do you want me to make love to you?"

"Yes." She'd been wishing for it. She wondered what had taken him so long.

All of her doubts and suspicions left when he climbed between her legs and licked her pussy until her thighs trembled. He made her scream his name over and over until she just about went hoarse. The man knew how to lick a clit and suck one too. He was a freak and "Freak" was Brittany's middle name. She had finally met her match. The two screwed like two back alley cats, clawing and biting until they both finally exploded with one big orgasm.

Sex with Craig was what she expected and more. He was an experienced lover, and he made her climax again and again. He left her trembling and weak. She thought that she'd died and gone to Heaven.

* * *

Craig knew from Brittany's reaction to his lovemaking that he had her where he wanted her. He had sensed right off that she would be one of those simple-minded women. She might be smart in the head, but when it came to relationships, she was dumb. She was too blinded by love. Looking for love in all the wrong places; almost needy. But, it didn't bother him one bit. She'd just be another one that he'd love and leave.

He wanted to hold on to Brittany a little bit longer because his real girlfriend had started tripping. He didn't know how long Carmen would let him live with her and he might need to use Brittany for a place to stay until he worked things out.

Yeah, sure Brittany was nice and all. Weren't they all? More like stupid. He sure knew how to pick them. All he had to do was look for the least attractive women. Most of them had something that they could work with. Brittany had a fine ass body. And on top of that her pussy was tight and her head game on point. But, she was no beauty queen.

Craig smiled as he lay in the bed next to Brittany. He had sexed her down and now she slept like a Siamese cat. He hadn't even had to wear a condom. She'd told him about being on the shot. He liked that. He liked getting it raw whenever he could.

Brittany had seemed like an insatiable nymphomaniac. Her pussy had felt moist and hot, as she'd kept gripping him with her muscles. He had nutted three times and would have kept going if he hadn't caught a cramp.

Yeah, he could slide up into Brittany's freaky ass anytime. If she let him fuck her without a condom, she might swallow his jism. That shit would be so righteous. He got hard again just thinking about it.

Carmen never gave him head because she thought putting her mouth on a dick was nasty. She always rationed her pussy and didn't do anything freaky either. When he did get some, it only lasted one round. If he wanted more, he had to jack off. That's why he had to cheat.

Brittany wasn't the first one and she wouldn't be the last. He might find sexual gratification elsewhere, outside of his relationship, but Carmen was the woman he loved. That's the way it was. Brittany may think that she'd found Mr. Right, but she hadn't. That's why you shouldn't go looking for love in the nightclubs.

Craig lay back on the bed and clicked on the TV. He had a self-satisfied smirk on his face. When would the women ever learn? What looks good to you ain't always good for you. He would ride this wave as long as the ocean remained calm. When the turbulent waters roared in, he'd be out of there like a male stripper being forced to pay child support for ten kids.

Chapter Eight

*O*n Friday, Camille sat home alone. She didn't bother to cook dinner because Dexter had already called to inform her that he'd be late. He and the guys had gone to the sports bar after work to unwind. She didn't care. Him and his damn sports. She wondered if Meredith Walker would be at the sports bar. Damn her.

She felt so depressed. What if Dexter really was interested in Meredith Walker? There would be nothing that she could do to turn the situation around. She felt unattractive and ugly. Did her moods and outbursts push Dexter away or did her body? Maybe the sight of her repulsed him? Her stomach protruded more and she saw the beginning of stretch marks on her thighs. At that moment, she hated being pregnant.

She sat in front of the television and watched a movie on *Lifetime*. The movie turned out to be about an unfaithful wife. It only depressed her more after it ended.

She switched to another station and went to the kitchen to get the Oreos. She poured a tall glass of milk to go with the cookies.

As she stuffed her face, she couldn't stop thinking about Dexter and wondering what he was doing. Was he really at the sports bar? She picked up the cordless and dialed his cell phone number.

"Hello?" He answered on the third ring.

"Dexter, it's me."

"Yeah?" He had an annoyed tone in his voice.

"I'm not feeling well. Do you think you might make it home soon?"

"I don't know." He didn't sound too concerned. She could hear loud cheering in the background, so she figured he really was at the sports bar. That didn't stop her mind from conjuring up images of Meredith, though.

"You don't know, or you don't care?" she snapped.

"Camille, can't I even enjoy a night out without you spoiling it? I'm so tired of you hounding me with your suspicions. I'm not doing anything. Damn."

"I didn't say that you were."

"Well, stop calling me every fifteen minutes, then. I am at a sports bar, watching the game. There's no one here with me except a bunch of hairy ass men. We are eating hot wings and drinking beer, looking at sports. That's what you do at a sports bar, Camille. Now, if you don't mind, I would like to get back to the game. Bye." He promptly hung up on her.

Camille didn't know what she had expected to accomplish by calling him. She had known that he wasn't going to come home until he was good and ready. And why should he come anyway, to hear her rant and rave? If he did come, he would be in one part of the house and she in the other. They'd barely spoken since her blow up the night before.

She didn't know why she got so emotional. She wanted her body back, her life back, and her husband back.

She picked up a pillow and fluffed it. Her back really did hurt, but she wasn't feeling sick. She took a Tylenol and tried to sleep. She leaned against the pillow and cried silently.

Dexter spotted Camille on the couch when he finally did get home. It was late, after two o'clock. He eased the door closed, trying to be extra quiet. He had tied on one too many beers and could feel it. He didn't need to end the night arguing with his wife. He stood there for a minute and stared at her as she slept. He hated feeling the way he did. It made him so angry that his wife didn't trust him. It also hurt. What could he do to prove his faithfulness? Stay away from Meredith? Fire her? He still didn't think that either of those options would satisfy Camille. She'd find something else to nag about.

"Hey," he nudged her gently. "Go get in the bed," he told her quietly. "I know you can't be comfortable on the couch." He knew he damn sure wasn't last night or all the other nights that he'd slept there. Leather got hot and sticky when you sweated. He wasn't looking forward to the couch.

Camille got up, but she didn't say anything to him. He could tell that she'd cried herself to sleep from the streaks on her face. She held her back as she walked slowly out of the room.

Dexter sighed, sat down and took off his shoes. He remembered what his adoptive father had always told him: "Never let the sun go down on your anger, son." At that moment, he felt like he'd failed his father. Hell, he couldn't even pacify his own wife.

"Ain't this a bitch," he said, and punched the pillow. A change had to come.

* * *

"Camille, you and I have got to talk," Dexter told her Saturday morning. His back hurt like hell from sleeping on the couch. He absolutely refused to sleep anywhere else, except in a bed that night and all other nights.

"It's pointless, Dexter. All we do is argue and you never want to hear what I have to say," she told him. She lay in bed on her side with a pillow supporting her back.

"Maybe I'd listen if you'd try to be reasonable and stop yelling and accusing me of doing things. I understand that you're pregnant and that your body is going through all kinds of changes, but damn," he shook his head, "It's like I'm being attacked constantly. I can't do anything right. Now, I'm supposed to be cheating on you, just because I took my secretary to lunch?" Dexter stopped abruptly. He realized that he'd said too much, but it was already too late.

Camille sat up in bed. Her eyes flashed with ill-concealed anger. "You took her to lunch? When Dexter? You never mentioned taking her to lunch?" Dexter looked down at his feet, avoiding eye contact with his wife. He knew he had messed up.

"Yes, I did. I did take her to lunch a few times," he admitted, seeing no reason to try to cover up or lie since he'd already let the cat out of the bag.

"A few times? Exactly how many times, Dexter?" He could tell by the look on her face that he'd upset her again. Pretty soon she would be so out of control, that there would be no reasoning with her.

"Camille, me taking Meredith to lunch in not the issue," he began.

"How the hell do you figure that? Of course it's the issue. The reason that I'm so upset is because you're never here. You're never here because you're probably out whoring around with her."

"Our problems started before Meredith ever came on the scene," he reminded her.

"Well, her appearance certainly hasn't helped things, now has it?" she asked sarcastically.

"Why can't you just admit that maybe you've changed, Camille? Maybe that's why we're having so many problems."

"Of course I've changed. I'm pregnant," she snapped.

"You're just using that as an excuse. You were never this jealous and insecure before we got married," he pointed out.

"And you haven't changed?" she questioned. "I guess you're just Mr. Perfect? You think it's easy being pregnant? You think I like being sick and swollen and bloated? You think I like being on this emotional roller coaster everyday? Huh? Well, Dexter, if you don't want the baby, I can take care of that."

"What exactly do you mean?"

"It's not too late for me to get an abortion," she yelled.

A deathly silence fell over the room. Dexter stood there, shocked beyond belief. He couldn't believe what he'd just heard.

Suddenly, anger seized him. He crossed the room in quick strides and glared down at his wife.

"Are you out of your fucking mind? You are not going to kill my child," he said passionately. "And don't you ever, ever consider that an option. I hope you don't think that I would condone something like that. That is my blood too." His eyes flashed.

Camille shrank back from him. She had never seen such a display of fury from her husband. It scared her. If she didn't know Dexter well enough, she would have thought that he'd actually put his hands on her.

Dexter caught the look of fear on her face and backed away.

"Camille," he said more quietly. "I know that we're going through a phase right now, but I think that once the baby comes, everything will be okay." He tried once again to reach her with his words. He wanted what he said to break down the barriers between them. He continued talking. "No matter how bad things seem, Camille, I swear to you, I have not cheated on you." Their eyes locked.

"Yet," she finally tossed at him.

"See, that's what I'm talking about." He pointed at her. "Why can't you just let it go, Camille?" Dexter threw up his hands. "I just can't deal with this." He walked over to the closet and reached up to the top shelf. He pulled down two suitcases and tossed them on the bed. "You don't have to worry about kicking me out of this bed anymore. I'll be staying at a hotel." He opened the first suitcase and began putting some of his personal belongings into it.

"Dexter, you're not leaving me, are you?" Her voice shook. She sat up in the bed.

"I'm going to give you some space, because I refuse to be put through all of these changes just because you're going through them."

"You can't just walk out on me. I need you," she told him, feeling a panic attack overcome her.

"No you don't." He walked over to the dresser and pulled out underwear and socks. "I don't know what you need, but it's not me. If you needed me, you wouldn't keep pushing me away." He finished packing his clothes and went into the adjourning bathroom. He came back out with his razor, after-shave, toothbrush, and other personal items. He threw them into the second suitcase with his undergarments.

"Dexter, please don't go," Camille pleaded. "I don't want to be in this apartment by myself." He continued to pack. "You made a promise to me when we got married. You promised to stick by me for better or worse. Didn't those words mean anything to you?"

He paused, choosing his words carefully. "Camille, those vows meant everything in the world to me. If they didn't, I never would have said them." He exhaled. "But, I can't live like this. We will work things out, but we need to put some distance between us. If we don't, then our marriage just might be over." He spoke honestly, zipping the suitcase.

"I'm sorry, Dexter," she said softly. Her bottom lip began to tremble. "Please-" She reached over and grabbed his arm as he picked up the suitcases.

"Don't, Camille. It's the only way. We can't keep hurting each other." He stared into her eyes. "Let's take this time apart to reevaluate our feelings; to find out if being married is what we really want."

"All I want is you, Dexter. You know that." He moved away from her and headed toward the door. She got off the bed, rushed over to him and threw her arms his waist. "Dexter, don't go. Don't do this to me. Please."

"I'll call to check on you and to let you know where I'll be staying." He tried to pry her arms away, but she held on firmly.

"No. Don't leave."

"I have to." He hugged her against his chest as she cried hysterically. It tore him up on the inside, but he remained adamant about leaving. They could not continue to coexist under the same roof with so much tension between them.

Chapter Nine

*T*he burden of what he'd done lay heavy on Dexter's heart. When he'd finally left, Camille had still been crying. He just could see no other way. If he stayed in that apartment with her, he couldn't be sure what might happen.

In his thirty-two years, he'd never become violent towards a woman. One thing that the Grays had taught him was to respect women and treat them like queens. He couldn't believe that he'd felt the urge to choke his wife when she'd told him that she could get an abortion. He'd felt the rage and had backed off. That's the reason that he'd had to get away. He would never lift a finger to hurt his wife, but why stay and keep fueling the fire? Just the thought of considering putting his hands on her, scared him damn near to death. Leaving was the best thing.

Dexter checked into a Holiday Inn on the beach and then he called his best friend, Walter. Walter had stood in as best man at his wedding. They hadn't talked in a few weeks, but that was all good. They both understood that the other had a hectic lifestyle.

Walter lived in Atlanta. He owned a graphics design business. He also played the saxophone for a major, jazz band in his city. He spent his spare time working in his in-home studio, producing and writing music for a variety of local groups. So, Dexter knew that his friend had a very tight schedule. But Walter would never be too busy to talk to his best friend.

"So, how's it going, my brotha?" Walter's voice filled with cheer. He seemed happy to hear from Dexter.

"Trouble in paradise," Dexter told him.

"Aw man. Already? Dexter, my brotha, whacha doin' wrong?"

Dexter didn't go into great detail about what was happening in his marriage, but he did tell Walter the basics. He told him about Camille's moodiness, her constantly riding him about where he went. He also mentioned Meredith Walker and how Camille thought that he had cheated with her.

"So, do you think that separation is the thing to do?" Walter asked after listening to his homeboy. "You sure you want to do this, man?"

"Yeah. I mean, Walt, Camille has been off the chain this past month. You just don't know. Besides, it's only temporary."

"I'm sorry to hear that, man. But y'all gonna work things out. The first year usually is a hard year, but I guess in your situation, it's gonna be twice as hard, since she's pregnant too." He paused for a second. "So, tell me something?"

"Yeah?"

"This Meredith Walker-"

"What about her?"

"You have feelings for her? You think you might want to bone her, man?" Dexter cracked up. Walter had no kind of tact. That was just his way.

"Walt, you are stupid." He continued to chuckle.

"Well?"

"Man, I admit," he cleared his throat. "Honestly, I felt a small attraction towards her in the beginning. But that's over," he spoke truthfully. "I love Camille."

"You tell her?" Walter asked.

"Tell her what?"

"Did you tell her that you love her, Negro? You know how you can be."

"Naw, not lately," he admitted.

"Well, tell her, Man." Walter advised. "Women are all sentimental like that. They need to hear that stuff. Especially right now. Camille's pregnant. She's probably feeling unattractive. I heard that they get like that, man. Extra sensitive. You know, all that stuff they discuss on Oprah."

"Oprah, man you watch Oprah? You going soft on a brother or what?"

After Dexter finished his conversation with Walter, he thought about everything. Talking to Walter made him think back to his growing up years. Dexter really didn't like to dwell on the past because that wouldn't change it. He figured that he'd endured a great deal at an early time in life, which enabled him to be a stronger person.

Dexter's biological mother had given him up for adoption, as an infant. He had grown up in foster homes all of his life. He went in and out of different homes, not quite fitting in anywhere. Dexter hadn't found out until age eighteen that his biological mother was Hispanic and his father was Black. That kind of explained why he'd felt like he'd been too Black for the White families and too White for the Black families. His identity crisis had left him confused. As a teenager, he personally identified himself as a misfit, not really belonging to any race. A misfit was a danger to society. He had landed in a gang, with others like him and ultimately, he'd ended up at The Boys' Home, a permanent shelter for unruly, disruptive teens that had no one. He'd lived at The Boys'

Home for over a year until the Grays came along. Dexter got adopted into the Gray family at age fifteen. The Grays had shown him nothing but love and had given him the best. However, a part of him had always remained cold and empty. It was the part that missed his biological mother, the part that wondered why she had given him away. He had never felt comfortable expressing love to anyone. Deep down, he'd felt unlovable. Sure, he'd had plenty of women sexually, but he couldn't commit to any of them. But, Camille had entered into his life and had changed his way of thinking, believing and feeling. She had loved him unconditionally. He'd finally felt like a whole person for the first time in his life. Dexter remembered the day that he'd met her.

He'd gone to Tyrone Square Mall to shop. He'd ended up in the department store looking for Curve cologne. It was for Walter's upcoming birthday. He knew that Walter used it like water and it was something that he could just ship to him overnight.

"May I help you, Sir?" a soft voice asked.

Dexter turned and stared into the face of an angel. She was dressed in a simple outfit, yet she appeared elegant. She smiled, showing perfect, white teeth and dimples.

"Er, do you have curves?" he'd asked. She'd giggled at the slipup. "I mean Curve. Curve cologne for men," he'd corrected, quickly.

"Well, yes. I do," she'd answered. "I mean we do. Have Curve, that is." They'd both laughed.

He'd glanced at her nametag. Camille Washington. She was very pretty, with a dark, chocolate, smooth skin tone. Her hair was simply styled in a wrap. It was long like the singer Aaliyah's.

"Will that be all for you today?" she'd asked.

"Yes, that'll be it," he'd said. She'd rung up his purchase and placed it in a small bag. She'd handed him his change and receipt.

"Thank you for patronizing our business. Please come again," she said politely.

Dexter walked away, but he couldn't stop thinking about her smile. He'd gotten halfway out of the mall when he turned around and went back to the department store. He sought out Camille.

"Hello?" She'd looked surprised to see him again so soon.

"I need your help," he'd stated.

"Well, sure. Did you need to have your cologne gift wrapped?"

"No, actually, I need help writing down a phone number- yours."

"Well, I don't usually give my number out to strangers," she'd said shyly, but he could tell by the look in her eyes that she was pleased he'd asked.

"My name is Dexter Lee Gray," he'd introduced himself.

"Camille Washington," she'd offered.

"So, now that we're no longer strangers-" he'd teased.

"I don't usually do this," she'd begun. "But, I guess it'll be okay." She started writing it and stopped suddenly. "You're not married, are you?"

"No. I'm a single bachelor. What about you?"

"I'm single too," she'd confessed.

"By choice, I bet?" he'd flirted.

"Well, men usually don't call me back after the first or second date," she'd confessed.

"Really?" Dexter found that hard to believe. "Why? You got some secret that would make a good Jerry Springer episode?" She'd laughed.

"No."

"You have enough kids to form your own basketball team?"

"No," she'd shaken her head and laughed again.

"Well, I can't imagine why someone would leave you single and available. But I'm so grateful to all those guys."

Dexter smiled, as he remembered their first date. That's when he'd discovered why Camille was single. She'd shared that she was a virgin and that most of the guys that she'd dated, gave up when she wouldn't let them get past first base.

In Dexter's opinion, those men had to be straight stupid. He felt that being a virgin was an honorable thing. He didn't try to con her into giving up her virginity or pressure her. He'd treated her like the queen that she was and in time, he'd earned her trust. Before long, she'd not only given him her virginity, she'd also given him her heart. Both of those constituted the most precious gifts he could ever receive.

Now, they'd come to a standstill in their marriage. Dexter was alone in a hotel room and Camille was alone at their apartment. Both of them, left to wonder about the other.

Chapter Ten

*J*ust as April had predicted, Darren waited for her. He sat at her apartment, leaned back against the door, asleep. She couldn't get in her door without going past him.

"Wake up." She was pissed at him for embarrassing her at the club. "Why the hell you sitting out here? My neighbors will probably report this to the leasing office. I can't afford to get kicked out of here.

They're already tripping about renewing my lease. Get ya ass up and go home."

"I ain't goin' nowhere. I'm comin' in wit' you." He staggered to his feet as April unlocked the door. He leaned to the side, lost his balance, and fell into her. Both of them tumbled over into the apartment.

"Damnit, Darren. Get off me." She got up, pulling her dress down, trying to cover up her thongs. She shut the door, hoping that none of her nosey neighbors were up at that time of night to witness what had happened.

"April, come here." Darren still lay on the carpet.

"No. I told ya ass to leave. So, if you want to stay, you can sleep right there." She left him on the floor.

"April, come on, now. Jus' help me up."

"Did I help ya ass get down there? No." She went into her bedroom and shut the door. She was tired and wanted to sleep. April knew it would be hard to make it to work on time, if she made it at all. She took off her club clothes, which smelled like smoke. She thought about taking a shower but she didn't have the energy. She pulled on her nightgown and got in the bed forgetting all about Darren in the next room.

She was half sleep when she heard the knob turn. Her eyes snapped open. Damn. She hadn't locked the door. She knew that Darren would try to get some. She was not in the mood.

"April, why you lef' me out there?" he slurred. She felt him sit on the edge of the bed, more like fall on it in his drunken state.

"Darren, don't mess with me tonight. I have to go to work in the morning. I don't have time for your shit."

"You ain't got to get no fucking attitude. You jus' mad 'cause I broke that shit up between you and that Busta at the club."

"It ain't like you did nothin'. I can talk to whoever I want. You don't own me."

"Maybe I don't. But that right there, belongs to me." He patted her in her private area, which infuriated her further. He began to rub her thigh under the sheet.

"Get ya damn hands off me." She threw his hand off. "I don't want you touching me."

"What? I know you ain't tripping. You don't want me touching you, but some other man can? That's real fucked up, April. You need to 'plain that shit to me, 'cause I don't understand."

"I ain't got to explain nothing to ya drunk ass. Now leave me alone. I'm going to sleep."

"You sleep when I tell you to."

"You must have bumped ya head or something." April sat up, forgetting to be tired. Darren had lost his mind and it was time for her to put her foot down. "I pay the mothafucking rent here. What the fuck do I look like? You don't come up in my shit tripping. You need to leave with that bullshit."

"I'm not going nowhere." Before she knew what happened, Darren had pulled her back down on the bed and lay across her.

"Get off me."

"No. Now, stop tripping. I told you, you belong to me." He kissed her forcefully. She could taste the stale liquor on his breath.

"Darren, stop."

"No. You can't make me stop." He overpowered her. She felt him spreading her thighs apart with his knees. She couldn't believe that he was behaving like a maniac.

"Darren, I said no." She pounded on his back, but he just shrugged her licks off.

"And I said, you don't tell me no." He pushed her gown up to her waist and penetrated her swiftly. It happened so fast that she couldn't catch her breath. He kept kissing her, putting his tongue down her throat, smothering her words of protest. He pumped in and out quickly. Within seconds he moaned and laid still, soon snoring loudly.

April pushed him off and went into the bathroom. She turned on the light and saw that her neck had hickeys everywhere. She had bruises all over her arms and upper body where Darren had handled her extremely rough. She felt dirty, humiliated and used. She felt like a piece of meat.

She didn't want to think about what had just occurred. The word rape entered her mind, but she quickly squirted away from it. I mean, your son's father, couldn't rape you, could he? She just didn't want to associate what had happened with something so ugly. She summed it all up to Darren being so wasted that he hadn't realized what he'd done. Thank God she was on that Depo shot or she could have gotten pregnant for sure. The last thing she needed was another illegitimate child from a low-life, jobless, asshole like Darren.

April arrived late to work the next morning. Her manager frowned at her as she walked past her cubicle to get to her work area. She knew that she would get called into her office. Her strict manager played by the rules. Just as she'd expected, she got a pop up email as soon as she turned her computer on. It was from her manager. She wanted to see April, as soon as possible.

"So, tell me what's going on, April?" her manager began, as soon as she took a seat.

"I just couldn't make it on time this morning," April answered.

"Is there anything in particular that's keeping you from getting here? Are you having some type of situation that you would like to discuss? Maybe I can be of some assistance." April stared at her blankly. What the hell could she do? She needed to just mind her own business. April truly felt that her manager signaled her out. She wasn't the only person that was late. She wished the wench would get off her case.

When it became obvious that April wasn't going to offer any response, her manager frowned. "You leave me no choice but to mark you as tardy. You know that if you are tardy again, I'll have to mark it as an occurrence." April didn't give a damn about an occurrence. She just wanted to go to sleep. Her head hurt, and she couldn't stop thinking about how horrible Darren had behaved.

The manager went on and on about how occurrences affected their raises and so forth and so on, but April had already tuned her out. It definitely would be a long day.

Chapter Eleven

*C*amille woke up the next morning determined not to shed one tear over Dexter. If he wanted to throw their marriage away, so be it. She was still young. She could find someone else. She knew there were some men out there who would accept her, even if she did have a child.

She fixed breakfast, which consisted of oatmeal, fruit and milk. She wanted to eat healthy for the baby's sake. She also made sure that she took her prenatal vitamins. She needed her energy to begin her new job at the insurance agency. Even though she was having marital problems, she wouldn't let it interfere with her job. Now, more than ever, she needed to work.

She felt slightly nauseous even after eating, but she figured it would pass. She took a bag of almonds to nibble on, in case the nausea didn't reside right away. She didn't want to be sick on her first day. She knew it had probably been brought on by stress.

She hadn't slept much last night. She'd kept replaying the argument she'd had with Dexter over and over in her head. She felt that she had every reason to be angry with him. How could he have lunch with his new secretary and not tell her anything about it? It was like keeping a secret. Then, he'd left their home in the middle of the night to take that same woman home. He'd said that it was because she'd locked her keys in her car and had to get the spare. Whatever. She'd heard about how women used that dumb tactic to reel men in. Could Dexter be that naïve or could he actually be interested in Meredith Walker?

She couldn't help thinking that she'd pushed her husband away with her childish tantrums. Just because she was pregnant, she wanted to have Dexter home with her every day. It was unreasonable. Maybe he felt stifled. Just because two people got married, didn't mean that they couldn't have a life outside of their marriage. Dexter had friends and co-workers before he'd even met her. It would be unfair for her to ask him to drop those friendships because they'd gotten married. She'd also had friends before she'd met him. However, all of her friends were in California. She hadn't seen them in a couple of years, since she'd moved away to attend USF in Tampa.

She liked Florida and had decided to stay. She was one semester away from receiving her Bachelors degree in Human Services. She already had an A.S. in Sign Language Interpretation, but hadn't located anything in that field since she'd received her degree. Once the baby was born and she had him or her in daycare, she'd pursue her education further. She felt that education truly was the key and you could never learn too much.

She decided not to call Dexter even though she felt tempted. It would probably only aggravate the situation further. She'd give him the space that he needed. If he decided to return to her, that would be fine. If he felt that they should separate, she didn't know how she'd deal with it. She'd cross that bridge if she came to it.

Camille got dressed. She knew that the dress code was casual. The temp agency had sent her some paperwork, which included timesheets, directions, etc. She put on some beige slacks. They had lots of pockets. It seemed that pockets were the in thing nowadays.

She wore a navy blue, cotton shirt. She'd take a sweater in case it was cold in the building. A lot of big corporations kept it freezing.

Camille made it through the first part of orientation with no problem. They gave them an hour for lunch, which was a treat. Their normal lunch would only be thirty minutes. She went to the cafeteria and got some steamed broccoli, meatloaf and mashed potatoes. The guys behind the counter were friendly. A tall, cute Italian guy rang up her order. The black guy kept staring at her and grinning. He was missing about three teeth in the front, but that didn't stop him from being courteous and cheerful.

Later, after orientation, the supervisors escorted the temporary employees over to the building where they'd be working. They explained the job assignment to them. It involved processing insurance claims for three different states: Florida, New Jersey and New York. Since New Jersey and Florida had the heaviest volume of claims, the Medical Billings department had fallen behind. The company had hired temps for that reason. They'd all be working for at least six months. After three months, if they wanted to become permanent employees, they could apply.

The job seemed pretty easy. Camille sat next to a processor named April Dillard and watched her enter claims. It wasn't long before four o'clock had rolled around.

"So, you think you're coming back?" April asked.

"Yes, I'll be back."

"It's not so bad. You'll catch on in no time," she told her. "I think you'll be sitting in that empty seat in front of Brittany." She pointed over to where a dark skinned girl sat. She noticed them talking and came over.

"Hi," she said to Camille. "I'm Brittany Anderson."

"Hello. I'm Camille Gray."

"So, you think you're going to like it here?" Brittany asked.

"So far," she replied.

"It's easy. Everyone is cool. The managers don't really bother you much. It's just a lot of nosey people who need to mind their own business, though."

"I know that's right." April laughed.

"Plus, I have to warn you about Craig right away. Are you married?" she asked.

"Yes," Camille answered.

"That doesn't matter. Craig tries to hit on every woman in a skirt, pants, or Capri's." They all laughed. "Just ignore him. Once you start talking to him, he will never go away."

"He's that guy with the big stomach over there talking to Brad," April told her. They turned to look.

"Isn't Brad a manager?" Camille asked, curiously.

"Yes. He is so fine, ain't he?" Camille had to agree. Brad was tall, medium to slim built, with smooth, brown skin.

"Brittany wants to get with him," April told her.

"I won't lie, I sure do," Brittany said, without shame. "Everyone around here does."

Brad seemed to sense that they were talking about him. He glanced over and smiled. They all giggled.

"He knows he's got it going on. Look at him." They watched as he walked over to talk to one of the other managers. "He is too fine."

"Hey, let me get out of here. It's a quarter after. I got to pick up my kids," April told them, getting up to take her left over work to a team leader.

"You have any children?" Brittany asked Camille.

"Not yet. But I'm pregnant."

"Oh really?" Brittany exclaimed. "You don't look pregnant."

"I'm only three months," she explained.

"That's great. I have two boys and April has a boy and a girl. Speaking of children, I have to go pick mine up, too."

"Well, it was nice meeting you," Camille told her.

"You too. You'll be sitting by me, so I'll show you the ropes. See you tomorrow."

"Bye."

Camille received a surprise when she got home. Dexter had bought her roses. They sat in the center of the table; a beautiful, floral arrangement, that filled the room with their scent. Smiling, and with her heart in her throat, she went over and picked up the card with trembling hands. It read:

"Baby, I know it's hard but things will get easier. Congratulations on your new job. I miss you and I love you. We'll work this out. Love, Dexter."

Reading the note brought tears to her eyes. She wanted to feel her husband's arms around her so badly at that moment. She missed him so much. She needed him there, but knew that he shouldn't be home if it wasn't where he wanted to be.

She sighed. She had absolutely nothing to do. She didn't have a husband to cook dinner for. She didn't even have his dirty laundry to wash. Everywhere she went in the apartment it reminded her that Dexter wasn't there anymore, making her sad.

Camille undressed, put on her nightgown and lay across the bed. She turned on the TV. It was on an urban station that played music videos. She heard the soulful sounds of Maxwell singing a song entitled *Lifetime*. As she listened to

the lyrics, the tears came. Would she and Dexter have a
lifetime together or would Meredith Walker's interference
break them apart forever?

Once again she thought about putting a face with the
name. Something inside of her urged her to find out
Meredith's identity. But, she wasn't a vindictive person. At
least, she'd never thought she could be one. Deep down,
somewhere in her heart, she wanted to hurt Meredith Walker.
After all, she was the reason that Dexter wasn't home where
he belonged.

Camille got up and went into the living room where the
caller ID box was located. On impulse, she searched all the
numbers in the memory looking for one particular name. It
wasn't long before she found what she wanted.

Without giving herself time to rationalize, she dialed the
number for Meredith Walker.

"Hello?" The voice on the other end seemed to be
irritated. Camille wanted to say something, but the words
stuck in her throat. "Hello?" the woman repeated.

Camille cleared her throat. "Hello. Is this Meredith
Walker?" she finally managed to get out.

"Yes."

"I want to know one thing, are you sleeping with my
husband?"

Nothing but complete silence came from the other end.

"Who is this?" Meredith questioned, after getting past the
initial shock.

"Camille Gray. I want to know if you're having an affair
with my husband, Dexter Gray?"

"Look, I don't have time for games," Meredith snapped.
"Don't you trust your husband? Maybe you should follow

him or have *Cheaters* do it for you. At any rate, don't call me anymore." She hung up in Camille's ear.

"Bitch." Camille was livid. She slammed the receiver down. Who the hell did Meredith think she was questioning her about her husband? She was the desperate whore that lusted after a married man. Well, if Meredith thought that she could just walk in and take Camille's husband without a fight, she had another think coming.

Camille finally made up her mind. She would meet Meredith Walker and a confrontation would be inevitable. That trifling slut had pissed her off.

Chapter Twelve

Dexter knew that Camille had gotten the roses. He had put them on the table, so there was no way that she could miss them. He had expected her to call him but here it was nine o'clock at night and he'd heard nothing. He began to worry. By nine thirty he picked up his cell phone and dialed home only to get the answering machine. Maybe she had gone to sleep. He remembered that she went to bed earlier now that she carried a child.

He breathed a sigh of relief when he heard the phone to his hotel room ring. Maybe Camille had assumed that he'd turned his cell phone off and was calling the room. He picked it up.

"Hello?"

"Dexter, this is Meredith," the sultry voice on the other line said. It took a second for it to register that he wasn't hearing his wife's voice.

"Meredith? Why are you calling me?" He couldn't keep his disappointed from being evident.

"You don't have to sound so excited. You left the number to the hotel on my answering service, or did you forget?"

"Oh, yeah. Well, that was more so for Bill. So that he could contact me in case my cell phone can't get a signal. Anyway, can I help you with something?"

"Not really. I just wanted to let you know I got a call today from your little wifey," she purred.

"What?"

"I said your wife called me. Anyway, I didn't have time to chat. I was in the middle of a problem at my hair salon."

"What the hell did she call you for?" he demanded to know.

"You know, the usual. "Are you sleeping with my husband?" she mimicked. "Nothing major," she ended with a half laugh.

"Meredith, this is not a joke. You seem to be deriving pleasure from this situation. Well, it's not a game."

"You don't have to get mad at me, Dexter. It's not my fault that your wife is so insecure. You just tell her to stop playing on the phone. Can you do that? Can you?"

"Fuck you, Meredith," Dexter snarled.

"H-how dare you," she spluttered on the other end.

Dexter hung up on her. She was beginning to get on his nerves. He almost wished that he'd never met her.

Dexter paced the room. He could easily convince himself that Meredith had caused his marital problems, but that was not the case.

Just as he'd told Camille, the problems had begun before Meredith arrived on the scene. She had just escalated things when she'd begun pressuring Dexter with her sexual overtures. Because he'd experienced vulnerability and confusion, he hadn't resisted her like he should have. If he hadn't let Meredith get to him, she would have given up.

By not stopping it from the jump, he had almost encouraged her advances. Now he had to pay. But would the end of his marriage be the high price that he'd have to pay for his mistake?

Dexter thought about his anger towards Meredith and decided that it was uncalled for. He would have to make amends. Besides, she was his secretary. He couldn't have bad vibes flowing between them that his other employees might pick up on. He dialed her number and waited for her to answer.

"Hello?"

"Meredith, this is Dexter."

"Yes?" She didn't sound angry, as if she'd been waiting for him to call her back.

"I just wanted to apologize for blowing up at you. It wasn't your fault. None of this is your fault. I made my bed, now I'll just have to lie in it."

"You could be lying in my bed. You're over there in some lonely, hotel room and my bed is empty. It doesn't seem right," she said.

"Meredith, don't. I'm going through a tough time right now. You're not making things any better," he pointed out.

"Can you blame me, Dexter? From the moment that I saw you, I wanted you. I can't help it that I'm attracted to you. I want you so badly, that I ache. You may not admit it, but you felt some attraction for me too. It didn't just appear because of your marital problems. You still feel that attraction, Dexter. You want me just as badly as I want you."

"Meredith-" he sighed. "Why did I even bother to call you?"

"Because you couldn't resist," she teased. "Dexter, it will only take me fifteen minutes to be there. Just say the word and I'll be on my way."

"Meredith, just stop," he said again.

"Dexter, think about it. I know that you've had fantasies about me. I know that you were turned on by the thought of me wanting you. You're a man; one who needs to be taken care of sexually. Admit it Dexter. Why don't you just fuck me and get it out of your system? You want to."

Dexter was too amazed to be shocked by Meredith's brazen words. Hell, she had hit the nail right on the head. Since day one, he had thought about her constantly. He had thought about touching her fine, naked body and taking her like she wanted to be taken. He bet she liked it rough. Maybe she liked being slapped on the ass while he got it from the back. She might be the kind who liked to have her hair pulled and got turned on by dirty talk.

Dexter felt his pants begin to bulge in the middle. God. What the hell was he thinking. He was married. He couldn't let his mind stray to such lucid thoughts.

"Meredith, I have to go. I'll see you at work or whenever I run into you. Bye." He hung up.

His hands shook. What the hell had he started? How would he ever fix things between himself and his wife, when he wanted to commit adultery with another woman? Thoughts of him banging Meredith kept floating across his mind. He just had to get away before he made a big mistake and ruined his marriage for good.

Dexter woke up the next morning with an unrelenting headache. After his conversation with Meredith, he'd gone upstairs to the hotel's restaurant and tavern. He'd had one shot of Hennessey after the next. He'd only stopped drinking when the bartender had told him that they had closed for the night. He couldn't count the number of drinks he'd downed. He couldn't even remember how he'd gotten back to his room. He was so blitzed.

He felt nauseous but couldn't raise his head from the pillow in order to go to the bathroom. He prayed that he wouldn't vomit. He didn't need the added humiliation of lying in his own filth on top of everything else. The last time he'd felt so miserable happened the day after his bachelor's party. What the hell had possessed him to drink so recklessly?

Meredith Walker.

That realization only made his head pound harder. Somehow, he had to get Meredith out of his mind. If he slept with her would that do the trick?

He shook his head, which only compounded the pain. No. He couldn't do that to Camille. Besides, that would only complicate the situation further. If he did it once, what would make him stop from doing it again? What if he couldn't stop?

All of these thoughts ran through his mind.

Dexter had never considered himself to be a dishonorable man. He thought he wasn't the type that would ever be unfaithful. What made him so different from the cheaters? How was he so special? What set him apart from the rest?

He was no different. He was a man like any other man. Right now, he was a weak man. He knew that he needed to be strong in order to hold his marriage together. He wouldn't give in to his urges.

Dexter rolled over, managed to sit up then groaned.

"God." He ran his hands down the sides of his face, stopping to massage his temples. His stomach churned dangerously. He knew that if he didn't make it to the bathroom, he'd be paying to have the carpet cleaned. He rushed from the room.

Dexter sat on his knees in the bathroom and leaned over the toilet. Even after he'd vomited what seemed like all of his guts out, his head still pounded. He stared at the white, ceramic bottom of the bowl, wondering if anything else would come up.

After a while, it dawned on him that his headed wasn't pounding after all. It was the door. Somebody knocked relentlessly. He figured it had to be the maid and got up from the floor.

"Just a minute," he called out, hoarsely.

He saw his reflection in the mirror as he passed to open the door. Man, what a pitiful sight he made. His bloodshot eyes stared back and he needed to shave. He hoped that the cleaning woman didn't get too much of a shock when he opened the door.

He unlocked the latch and turned the knob. Meredith Walker stood in the hallway with a rose in her mouth. Dexter groaned aloud. Would the nightmare ever end?

Chapter Thirteen

April did not want to be bothered by Darren. Period. She kept thinking about what had happened between them the last time and just couldn't believe that drunkenness had prevented him from controlling himself. She felt that Darren had so little respect for her he thought of her as his property. She wasn't good enough to wed, but she was good enough to bed. Well, that had ended. Never again would she allow him to take control of her.

She set some new rules that he would have to abide by. First and foremost, he would have to take care of his son. She refused to continue to do it all by herself. If there weren't a change, she would be adamant about going through Child Support Enforcement. The outcome of the situation really would be left up to Darren. She told him as much the next time he came to pick up DJ.

Of course, Darren had reverted back to being sweet and mild mannered because he wasn't drunk. It didn't stop April from telling him what she felt, though. She wouldn't even let him past the front door. She talked to him with the security chain on.

"Darren, I don't want you coming to my house without calling first," she told him.

"What?" He stared at her like he thought she'd gone mad.

"You heard me. After what happened last time, I don't want you to just pop up any time you feel like it."

"My son lives here," he reminded her.

"But you don't."

"Man, you tripping."

105

"You the one who behaved like an idiot in the club and afterward."

"I didn't do nothin'."

"Of course not," she said sarcastically. "You never do."

"Why can't I come inside?" he whined.

"Because you think that I'm just some piece of ass that you can have whenever you want."

"It ain't even like that. You tripping.

"Save it Darren. It is what it is. I'm going to need for you to start giving me at least half of DJ's daycare payment each week," she continued.

"What?" he asked.

"Did I stutter?" She glared at him. "His daycare has gone up. I can't pay all my bills and his daycare too. I'm getting behind. I need some help."

"Well, why don't you get some of them men you screwing around with to pay your bills?" He said, trying to be hurtful.

"Why don't you get your bitch to pay your child support?" she threw back. "Since you ain't got a job?"

"I can get a job. I just don't see why you have to start tripping. I told you that I'd give you money for him if you needed it. You don't have to get the Man involved."

"I shouldn't have to keep reminding you," she pointed out. "You know he needs Pull Ups. You know he needs clothes. You know he needs shoes. You can see for yourself. I shouldn't have to beg you to provide for your son."

"I don't need to stand here and listen to you putting me down. It ain't like you do so much for him. You'd rather buy some outfit for the club before you buy something for ya kids."

April rolled her eyes at him, refusing to get into a heated argument. "Where's my son? You gonna let me get him or what?" he snapped.

"Wait a minute."

She closed the door and locked it. Darren stood on the other side amazed. She really wasn't going to let him in. After about five minutes the door opened and she threw a bag at him. Then, DJ came out. She slammed the door then reopened it to glare at him. "He need some more Pull Ups." she yelled before slamming it closed in his face, again.

"Ain't this a bitch." he muttered.

The door to the apartment adjacent to April's opened and a young man around Darren's age stepped out. He looked at Darren sympathetically, "Baby mama drama?" he inquired, like he knew the feeling.

"Like a mofo." Darren shook his head, picked up his son and left dejectedly.

On Friday night April had decided, on the spur of the moment, to go clubbing. She needed to unwind, have a few drinks and forget about her problems for a while. She called Brittany to see if she wanted to go to the club.

"Hey, what's up?" Brittany greeted.

"I was thinking about going out tonight. You want to go?"

"Yeah, but I don't have a babysitter."

"What about your lil' sister?"

"My mom is mad at me, so she's not going to let her come over. That's her way of paying me back."

"O-kay. Well, I'm leaving around eleven after I drop Peaches off at my mama's. Let me know if you get a babysitter."

"Alright. I'll call you on you cell if I change my mind."

"Okay," April told her and hung up.

That night April wore a silver dress with a low cut v-neck. Of course it was short and clingy. It tied around the neck in the back. She put on matching high heels.

As she headed towards the car, her cell phone rang.

"Hello?"

"It's Brittany, come pick me up. I'm going."

"Oh, you got a babysitter?"

"Well, yeah. Something like that."

"Alright. I'll be there in about ten minutes."

"See you."

Brittany wore a turquoise colored, pants suit. It fit her body like a second skin. Of course, her shoes matched. She'd gotten her hair cut into a low natural and she'd dyed it burgundy. She would definitely stand out in a crowd.

They headed for Tampa to the hot nightspots. The weekend was made for partying. They didn't want to miss out on any of the excitement.

"Did I tell you about what my baby daddy did?" April said, turning down the music that blasted from her system.

"No, what happened?"

"Remember the last time we went out? Well, he was waiting for me after I got home." April told Brittany the details of that night.

"No he didn't." Brittany's mouth hung open when April finished.

"Yes he did."

"Well, I guess you couldn't call the police. I mean, what would you tell them? They'd probably think it was a joke."

"Yeah. I know. Anyway, I told him that he can't come to my house no more without calling first. When he came to get Darren Jr., I didn't even let him inside. I just threw Darren's clothes at him and talked to him through a crack in the door."

"It's a shame. Well, I'm sorry to hear about your baby daddy drama. Things are going pretty well for me and Craig," Brittany bragged.

"Where is he tonight? I'm surprised he let you go out. You haven't been hanging lately," she said dryly.

"Well, he had to go out of town this weekend. He's in the Army Reserves," Brittany explained.

"At least one of us got a decent man," April remarked.

"Yes, Craig is one in a million. I lucked up this time around." She reached for her cell. "Hey, let's call Camille," Brittany said, changing the subject abruptly.

"The new girl from work?"

"Yeah, we should have invited her out."

"Isn't she pregnant? I don't think she'd want to hang at the club," April said.

"Well, it's not like she's showing yet. We could have asked her. I think she's having some problems with her husband. She might need to get out."

"Well, she can't drink."

"I know, but that doesn't mean she can't have fun," Brittany answered.

"She don't need to be around all that second-hand smoke. Not to mention all those drunk men who might try to paw on her."

April had her reservations. She personally felt that a pregnant woman had no business at a club. She always frowned when she saw women at the clubs with their stomachs poking out. If they couldn't wait nine months

before they started back being hoochie mamas, they should
have kept their legs closed.

Chapter Fourteen

*I*t was after eleven o'clock on a Friday night. Camille tried to read a romance novel but it didn't hold her attention. She couldn't sleep and didn't want to watch TV. Nothing could stop her from thinking about Dexter. She hadn't called him when she'd gotten the roses. She thought he'd have called her by now, but he hadn't.

When the phone rang, she assumed it would be him. It surprised her to hear from Brittany and April. They were headed for some club in Tampa. She could hear the excitement in their voices and felt envious of their freedom. If she weren't pregnant, she would be right out there with them. She thanked them for inviting her but declined.

After hanging up, she felt a wave of depression wash over her. She almost wished that she'd never gotten pregnant. It seemed to be a curse. She wasn't sure if she'd be in her present situation if she weren't carrying a child. Now that she thought about it, she doubted Dexter would have asked her to marry him so soon if he hadn't felt a certain obligation. If they had waited to get married, maybe they wouldn't be having all the problems they now had. A child complicated the situation.

If she weren't pregnant, she'd have responded to Dexter. She'd have tuned in to his needs. Then, he wouldn't have felt the need to stray and Meredith Walker would not be an issue.

Camille sighed loudly. She seemed to be sighing a lot lately. She'd never thought that the prospect of motherhood would be so draining. What type of mother would she make; she couldn't even keep her husband happy? Would she be able to take care of a child? If she and Dexter couldn't work past their problems, did she have the strength to do it alone?

She thought about her two newfound friends, April and Brittany. They were single parents raising two children by themselves. If they could do it, then she should be able to also. If she remembered correctly, April didn't get any child support and she managed to take care of her two. It was a struggle, but she was making it.

Camille was sure that Dexter would provide financial support for his child. That wasn't a concern. But, she didn't care about money. She wanted her family to be together.

Maybe once the baby came, she'd be able to express herself without all of the anger. Hopefully, she'd be able to reach him and make him understand that they belonged together. She loved him and wanted to be with him for the rest of her life. In her mind and heart she felt that marriage should be forever.

She tried to think of something to do that would shake the depression. Maybe the next say she'd go to the mall to shop for baby clothes and other items for newborns. When she glanced at her reflection in the full-length mirror, she changed her mind. She didn't want to be seen in public looking so bloated and unattractive.

Chapter Fifteen

April awoke in a state of alarm. If she arrived late to work one more time, she would probably get fired. She'd already received several warnings.

She couldn't stop the panic she felt. She needed her job. How would she pay the rent and car payments, not to mention the other bills that piled up daily?

"What you doing?" The question came from someone lying next to her.

"Getting ready for work." Who the hell had she picked up in the club? She was almost afraid to look. After she collected some courage, she glanced over at him. He looked vaguely familiar. She couldn't see his entire face because of the dreadlocks that blocked half of it.

"I thought you didn't work weekends?" It was the Jamaican guy that she'd met the previous week. God. How could she? What was his name?

"Weekend? What day is it?" She heard him chuckle.

"It's Saturday, gul. You mus' ta had too much to drink?" That was obvious. If she hadn't, he wouldn't have gotten lucky last night.

"Oh?" She breathed a sigh of relief and settled back down. If she thought that she would be able to get some sleep, she was wrong. The guy rolled on top of her.

"Give me some more of that good lovin' you give me las' nite," he told her. "You had my head spinnin', gul."

Did she have his head spinning or was it the amount of weed that he'd smoked? She vaguely remembered driving home in a cloud of marijuana fog. He'd been puffing and trying to past the joint to her.

She pushed him off of her. No way would she lay up under him while straight sober. What was his name? She racked her brain, trying to remember.

"I, um. I'm going to be sick," she lied and headed for the bathroom.

She stayed in there for at least fifteen minutes. When she came out, the guy was hanging up her phone.

"Some brotha jest called. He said he was bringin' ya son in fifteen minutes."

"Damnit." She couldn't believe that Darren would bring DJ home so soon. He'd just gotten him the night before. It wasn't right. He was supposed to keep him the entire weekend. Her anger made her forgot that a complete stranger had answered her phone. "Hey, you need to get dressed. Quick. I'm taking you home." It was a damned shamed. She couldn't even remember the guy's name.

"But he said he'd be here in fifteen minutes. You gonna jus' bail out on 'im like dat?"

"It ain't ya business. Now, if you wanna get back to Tampa, you better get dressed in a hurry or else you can call a cab because I will leave ya ass stranded."

"Damn, slow ya roll, gul." He apparently took her seriously because he quickly began to pull on his pants. April located his shirt and tossed it to him. What the hell was his name? How had he ended up in her bed when he clearly wasn't her type? As he pulled on his shirt, she caught sight of the tattoo he had around his belly button. What heterosexual man got a tattoo of the sun around his navel? She made a mental note not to ever pick up strangers again.

Chapter Sixteen

Brittany sat in front of Craig's grandmother's house for fifteen minutes, waiting on him. She rang the doorbell and knocked, but no one answered. Craig told her to pick him up at 7:00 because his car wasn't working. It was now 7:15 and he was nowhere to be found. She was getting irritated. Craig must be out of his mind to have her drive all the way to Brandon and not be where he'd said he was going to be.

Brittany got back into her car and decided to drive to his mother's house. She had visited once, but was certain that she could find it.

Maybe someone there would know where he could be located. It wasn't long before she found the house. She knew that it was the right one because Craig' car rested in the driveway.

She got out and followed the sidewalk leading up to the steps. She knocked several times and got no answer. Craig' entire family lived with their mother, including his two brothers, his sister, and her five children. She could hear music blasting and noise from televisions playing on different stations. She banged on the door.

"Who is it?" a voice finally called out.

"It's Brittany. Is Craig here?" she yelled.

"Wait a minute." She could hear someone call for Craig. "Come on in. He in the back. I'll get him." His younger brother, whom she'd met before, let her in. She'd actually met the entire family.

Brittany went inside and took a seat on the couch, trying not to stare at the filthy carpet. She could see different stains where one of the kids had spilled red KoolAid or soft drink of some kind. It could definitely use a good foam scrubbing. "Spraying a little Resolve on the stains wouldn't hurt either," she thought to herself. A good vacuuming, along with some carpet fresh would probably do wonders.

A little girl came over to her and held out her arms to be picked up. Brittany hadn't seen her before. She assumed that the girl was one of his sister's children. She picked her up.

"Hello, what's your name?"

"Jasmine," the child answered. She appeared to be around three years of age.

"That's a pretty name. My name is Brittany." It dawned on her that she'd heard that name before. Where? Then she remembered: on the social security card that had fallen out of Craig' wallet. She remembered that Craig had said that it was his sister's child.

"You have a cute daughter," she called to her.

"What?" The other woman turned from the movie that she had been watching on TV.

"I said, you have a cute daughter," Brittany repeated.

"Oh, that's not my daughter. That's Craig's lil' girl."

Brittany's mouth dropped open. "Craig's? He told me that he didn't have any kids," Brittany exclaimed.

The girl leaned back on the couch and roared with laughter. "Oh he did? Well, he lied. He got two kids: a son and a daughter. I don't know why he'd want to lie 'bout dat."

Shock settled over Brittany. She remembered that day when she'd asked him over and over if he had any children. He had lied to her with a straight face. The two social security cards had belonged to his children. She was furious. Craig had some explaining to do. He should consider himself lucky that she had enough respect not to start tripping in his mama's house.

Brittany held her peace all the way home. Craig could tell that something bothered her because she didn't say a word to him as they drove across the bridge. As soon as they got inside her apartment and the door closed, she slapped him across the face.

"What the fuck you do that for?" he asked confused. He rubbed his jaw where she'd hit him.

"You sister told me the truth. So, I know you lied about not having any children."

"I didn't lie," he protested, still rubbing his cheek. "Those are not my kids. At least, I don't think they're mine." Brittany glared at him. "Maybe Craig Jr. is, but Jasmine isn't. Do she look like me?"

"Craig, don't start. Don't even try that with me. If those children weren't yours, they wouldn't be living in your mother's house. She wouldn't have custody of them. What lies do you have to tell me about that?" He opened his mouth to speak, but she stopped him when she held up her hand. "You can just shut up because your sister filled me in on everything."

"My sister just be hating 'cause she got five kids and five baby daddies. You shouldn't believe nothing she say." No matter what, he wasn't going to admit anything. Brittany realized that Craig was a pathological liar.

"You know, you are pathetic," she told him. "Even when you're caught, you still can't stop lying. You have a serious problem. You're sick."

"I didn't mean to lie," he finally said. "I just didn't want you to think I was a deadbeat father because my kids live with my mama."

"What's so bad about that? Plenty of men I know don't have custody of their children. Why did you have to lie about it? There was no reason."

"I know. I'm sorry," he said stupidly. He looked at her with sad eyes.

"That's not going to work this time," she told him. "The sad, puppy dog face isn't going to get you out of this. I specifically told you, the last time we had a serious discussion, that I would not tolerate dishonesty."

Needless to say, her weekend had been totally ruined. She'd been nice enough to take Craig back home, but she had refused to accept his apology. She'd told him she felt it best that they ended things.

"I just can't deal with it. I mean, what will you tell a lie about the next time? I just don't want to go there." Craig actually looked as if he would cry when she'd dropped him off. Her heart had twisted, but she didn't give in.

Chapter Seventeen

Dexter stared at Meredith with a look of disbelief on his face. What had possessed her to just show up?

"Don't just stare, invite me in," she told him.

"Meredith, now is definitely not a good time," he said. He didn't care what she thought of him. At the moment, Meredith was the last person he wanted to see.

"Dexter, what's wrong?" Ignoring his dismissal, she entered the room. Because of the tightly closed blinds, darkness engulfed the entire room. "Why don't you let some light in here?" she asked.

"Don't," he said, when he saw her hand go for the cord to the Venetian blinds. "Please, don't open those," he said more gently, sitting on the edge of the bed.

"My, my, my." Meredith clicked her tongue, distastefully. "I think somebody tried to drown his sorrows last night. I guess you're paying the price this morning, huh?"

"Am I?" It was a statement, rather than a question.

"Well, you go in there and take a long shower. I'll put that coffee pot over there to use and we'll see what we can do about making you feel better," she instructed.

Dexter didn't understand why Meredith wanted to play Miss Susie Homemaker, but he didn't have the energy to protest. Coffee sounded like a good idea so he left the room.

Dexter ran the water as hot as it could get and let it cascade down on his aching body. He stayed in the shower until the water turned lukewarm. Amazingly, he began to feel human again.

When he returned to the bedroom, half-sober, stomach still queasy, he found that Meredith had made the coffee. She'd already poured some into a Styrofoam cup for him so he picked it up.

"Thanks," he mumbled. He took a swallow of the dark, bitter liquid. It was hot and felt good going down his throat, which felt raw from all the vomiting he'd done.

"So, what happened? You had to get drunk in order to convince yourself not to call me?" Meredith teased.

Dexter glared at her but didn't bother to respond. He stared at the rose, which lay next to him on the dresser.

"What's that for?" he asked. Her gaze followed his and rested on the flower.

"It's a peace offering." She walked over and picked up the rose. "I realize that I was wrong for calling you up and telling you about your wife. I apologize." She handed the rose to him. "I was out of line."

He stared at her in silence. He finally put his cup of coffee down, accepted the flower and leaned back against the dresser. "Apology accepted," he told her and sighed. "How did you find me?"

"It wasn't hard. The number showed up on my caller ID," she chuckled. "Oh, you think I'm some sort of a stalker?" Dexter didn't reply so she shook her head. "I'm afraid that's not my style."

That thought had crossed his mind. After all, he didn't really know much about her. He didn't want to get to know her. That could prove to be dangerous.

"Why did you come here, Meredith?" he ventured to ask. He stared at her, letting his gaze take in her lovely body. She had on a form-fitting, Capri outfit. She had abs of steel and the rest of her was toned to perfection. She even wore a ring in her belly button.

"Like what you see?" She didn't look away. "You can see everything, if you want." She licked her lips seductively.

"Don't start that again," Dexter stated.

"Stop pushing me away, Dexter. I know what I'm getting involved in. I don't have any fantasies about you leaving your wife for me. I don't even want that." She came and stood in front of him. "You don't have to worry about all the drama that usually takes place when a woman gets involved with a married man. I just want the physical intimacy." She ran one, perfectly manicured fingernail down the side of his biceps. Her slight touch felt like fire. Dexter trembled. "Come on, Dexter. We'll be discreet. No one has to know but us."

Dexter was so tempted. If he allowed himself just that one, little indiscretion, who would it hurt?

Meredith stood waiting for Dexter to make the call. Time seemed to stand still.

Finally, Dexter stepped to the side, breaking the closeness, the madness, releasing himself from her spell.

"Meredith. No." He released the breath that he held. "Like I said before, I love my wife. I will continue to honor my marriage vows. Just because I'm having problems, doesn't mean I should compound them by sleeping with you. I won't do it," he said with finality.

Meredith sighed loudly, frustrated. "Okay. Okay. I get the point," she finally said. "Well, it didn't hurt to try. You win some. You lose some."

Dexter glared at her. "What is this? Is it some sort of a game to you? You make a play at married men for a living?" he asked, sarcastically.

121

Meredith laughed. "Not at all. Actually, I just got out of a five year relationship." She paused, as if debating whether or not to continue with her story. A few seconds lapsed and she went on. "It was very abusive- mentally, physically and emotionally." She stared down at the floor, as if ashamed. "I haven't even been on a date since I broke up with Brandon." She chanced a glance at Dexter. "That was his name," she told him then continued. "He controlled every aspect of my life. I think he wanted me to be meek and humble, like one of those women you read about in the Bible. Well, I didn't fit that mode, so he tried to beat me into submission. I couldn't have an opinion of my own. He did all of the thinking for me. After we broke up, I swore I'd never get involved with someone so abusive and controlling ever again. I guess, somewhere, in the back of my mind, I figured that messing around with a married man would be safe. No strings attached."

Her confession shocked Dexter. He hadn't figured Meredith for the type to take any man's abuse. That proved that you just never knew people.

"I'm sorry to hear about what you went through," he offered.

"Well, it was an experience that I wouldn't wish on my worst enemy. "But-" She shrugged her shoulders. "I'm healing now. I'll get over it."

Dexter felt her pain. Underneath her tough, "I-don't-care attitude," Meredith hid her vulnerability and covered the hurt. He felt sorry for her. No one deserved to be used as a punching bag.

Instinctively, he went over and gave her a hug. It was a kind gesture, nothing more. Meredith, to his surprise, took it the way it had been intended.

She pulled away and smiled at him shakily. It took a while for her to compose herself. Dexter just waited in silence.

"Dexter, I feel so stupid," she finally admitted. "Can you forgive me? I've been behaving like a fool."

Dexter smiled, sheepishly. "Well, I guess you couldn't help yourself. I am irresistible."

They burst into laughter, easing the tension in the room.

"I wonder if your wife knows just how special you truly are," Meredith told him, once their laughter subsided. "I hope she appreciates you," she said with sincerity. "Not too many men would have turned me down."

Dexter knew that she had spoken the truth. He finished his coffee and suddenly felt ravenous. "Meredith, are you hungry?" he asked.

"Actually, I am."

"Let's go somewhere to eat, preferably a place where we can just sit and chill. I have a lot on my mind. If you don't mind me unburdening on you, I need to talk."

"That won't be a problem, Dexter. I know just the place," she said quietly.

"Okay. Well, lead the way."

Chapter Eighteen

Another wasted weekend, Camille thought as she flipped through a magazine. It was also one more day to regret that she'd caused her husband to leave. Usually, on the weekends, she and Dexter would do something together. That was, until the bickering had started. They would take in the latest movie or go out to dinner. Camille sure missed the family time they'd shared.

She had to pat herself on the back mentally, though. She had resisted the urge to call Dexter all weekend. She hadn't even thanked him for the roses he'd bought.

Maybe the roses eased his conscience. Could he be guilty of infidelity? Did he think that roses could erase all of the pain? If he'd cheated on her, she didn't care if those flowers wilted. They could shrivel up and die.

"I can't keep torturing myself with these thoughts. I need to do something," she said aloud. She found herself picking up the receiver. Instead of dialing Dexter's cell phone number, she forced herself to call her mother in California.

The phone rang three times. On the fourth ring the answering machine picked up.

"Hi, Ma. It's Camille. I was just calling to check on you guys. Tell Dad hello for me. I love you. Bye." She hung up after leaving the message. For some reason, she felt sad.

Maybe Brittany's home, she thought. *I'll call to see what she's up to.* Since she sat in the seat in front of Brittany at work, she and Brittany had gotten to know each other through conversations. Camille shared the fact that she and her husband had separated. Brittany had told her to call if she

124

ever needed to talk. Well, she needed to talk to somebody before she went crazy.

She got her address book and searched from the number she'd written down. She found it and dialed.

"Hello?" Brittany answered on the second ring.

"Brittany? Hello. This is Camille. I thought I'd call to see what you're doing."

"Nothing, girl. I'm still in bed," Brittany said drowsily.

"It's almost two o'clock in the afternoon," Camille pointed out.

"Remember, April and I went out last night. I had a fight with Craig, so I needed to get out and do something," she explained.

"What time did you guys get home?"

"Around four o'clock. I don't remember. April ended up taking some dreade-headed hoodlum home with her."

"What?" Camille asked, shocked. "Are you serious?"

"Yeah. She was drunk. I tried to talk her out of it, but she was too drunk to listen."

"That's horrible. I hope she was careful."

"Me too. Wait a second and I'll call her on three-way. Hold on." She clicked over and Camille waited.

"Hello?" April's voice came through, sounding gravely.

"Hey, April. It's Brittany and Camille."

"What's up?" she greeted.

"Nothing. We were wondering about you. So how was your friend from last night?" Brittany giggled.

"That shit ain't funny," April bellowed through the line. "Man, why you let me take that asshole home with me? You knew I was drunk. You supposed to have my back."

"But you're grown, remember? You kept telling me that all night when I tried to stop you." Brittany laughed and so did the other two.

"Well, you could have tried harder." April pouted through the phone.

"What's the problem? He wasn't any good in bed?"

"Girl, I don't even know. I can't remember shit. I don't even remember driving home," April admitted.

"I told her not to mix drinks, but she did that too," Brittany informed Camille. "She is a mess."

"So what y'all two up to? I want to go get something to eat," April told them, changing the subject. She didn't want to remember the stranger that she'd slept with. She felt almost ashamed of herself.

"Well, I am hungry. What about you, Camille?" Brittany asked..

"I'm pregnant. I'm always hungry," she answered. They cracked up. "Well, where y'all want to go? Any place in particular?"

"T.G.I. Friday," April suggested.

"Fine with me," from Camille.

"Cool," from Brittany.

"I'll pick you up in thirty minutes, Brittany. That'll give you time to get ready," April said.

"Okay. You pick me up. Then, swing through to get Camille. Where do you live, Camille?" She told them her address and they hung up.

An hour and a half later they sat at a table in T.G.I. Friday. All of their menus were opened as they tried to decide on what to order.

Brittany glanced up. "Damn," she exclaimed.

"What? You see something good? Where?" April asked, looking closer at the selections in front of her.

"It's not on the menu. It's walking towards us, getting ready to be seated," Brittany said silkily, licking her lips.

"Oh?" April took her eyes off the menu long enough to look. She had to do a double take. "He *is* fine. Look like that ball player, David Justice, that married Halle Berry," she whispered across the table.

Camille had her back turned to the man, so she couldn't see him. She didn't want to be so obvious and turn around. Apparently, the man must be incredible, the way Brittany and April drooled.

"He's sitting two tables behind you," Brittany told her. "When you get a chance, turn around and take a peek."

"No, I don't think so. I have a husband," Camille declined.

"Well, being married doesn't mean you don't have eyes," Brittany pointed out.

"True," April added.

"Are you ladies ready?" A waitress appeared and asked for their orders. She placed a basket of biscuits on the table.

"Yes. I am." This came from Brittany. The rest decided that they were ready as well. The waitress took their orders, then left. They all reached for a biscuit.

"These are so good," Brittany exclaimed.

"Yeah, they just melt in your mouth," April agreed.

"I've never tried them before, but they look delicious," Camille said, taking a bite. She nodded at them as she chewed. "They are delicious."

The subject soon turned to men. Brittany told them her latest story about Craig and his lies. The waitress returned within minutes with their salads and drinks.

Camille had asked for water. Brittany had ordered a gigantic Mud Slide and April had ordered a Strawberry Daiquiri. Camille envied them as she stared at their alcoholic beverages. It would be six more months before she could consume anything with alcohol.

"So, he does have children, but he said he didn't? Did he think he could keep it a secret forever? It's kind of hard to hide a lil' kid," April joked.

"What did he hope to accomplish by lying to you?" Camille commented. "Why didn't he just tell the truth when you first found those social security cards in his wallet?" She took a sip of her water and wished it could turn into a Strawberry Daiquiri. "So, what are you going to do?"

Brittany shrugged. "I don't know yet. I mean I really like him. We were talking about marriage," she confessed.

"Marriage?" April asked incredulously. "You just met him. You don't even know him."

"Well, you didn't know that guy that you let bone you last night," Brittany reminded her, cattily.

"That's different," April snapped. "Marriage is a big step. Plus, you're still married to your first husband. You gonna commit bigamy?"

"There is such a thing as a divorce," Brittany snapped. April rolled her eyes.

"Maybe you should reconsider since you've already experienced some problems," Camille intervened. "The last thing you want to do is make the wrong decision. You'll live to regret it." They fell silent and just sipped their beverages.

"Well, if we do get married, it'll be further down the line," Brittany finally spoke. "I didn't even take him back yet." She saw the waiter heading towards them. "Here's our food," she told them.

"Good, cause even after eating those biscuits and salad, I'm still starving," Camille exclaimed.

"Me too," April remarked.

They had almost finished eating when Camille remembered the guy that they'd discussed earlier. She had to admit, she was curious to see what he looked like. She turned halfway in her seat, trying to be inconspicuous.

When she saw him the blood rushed to her head, causing her to get dizzy. "Oh no," she gasped.

"What's wrong? Is it the baby?" Brittany asked in alarm.

"Camille?" April questioned. "Are you okay? Take deep breaths. Breathe."

"I'm fine. I mean, the baby's fine," Camille finally managed to say. "You're not going to believe this, but that fine guy that came in here earlier-" She paused and they waited impatiently for her to continue.

"Well?" Brittany urged.

"-that's my husband."

"What?" Both of them said simultaneously and stared at her in disbelief.

"And he's here with another woman. I'll bet you fifty bucks a piece that her name is Meredith Walker," she said stiffly.

"Who is that bitch?" Brittany questioned.

"She's his secretary," Camille answered in a sarcastic tone. Her eyes slanted showing her disgust and disapproval. "I can't believe he's here with her."

"They're just eating. It doesn't look like they're doing anything wrong," April pointed out.

"If I were you, I'd find out. I would not want my super fine husband to be out anywhere with another woman,"

Brittany told her. April and Camille stared at her. "Well, that's just the way I am. I would confront him. If he doesn't have anything to hide, he'll let you know," she told Camille. "Look at him with that Vanessa Williams-Fox Wannabe."

"Shut up, Brittany," April said, trying not to laugh. She knew that Camille was probably uncomfortable. She didn't know how she'd handle a similar situation. It was a strange situation to be involved in, like something from a soap opera.

"Just go. Do it. That's your husband." Brittany wouldn't let it go. "Investigate. Don't you want to know? Aren't you curious?"

Camille's mind whirled. She didn't know how to react. She didn't want to cause a scene and embarrass her husband, but she did want to find out if he was out with Meredith Walker. Her curiosity got the best of her.

Even though she got up from the table her feet seemed to be glued to the floor. She thought about just leaving it alone. She didn't need to complicate things any further, without all the facts. Then, as she looked on, the woman sitting with her husband leaned over and gave him a kiss.

That was all it took to get her legs moving. Within seconds, she stared down into Dexter's startled face.

"Camille, what are you doing here?" he asked, caught completely off guard.

"Maybe that's a question I should be asking you?" she snapped, her eyes blazing. His face seemed to lose its color right before her eyes. "You have some explaining to do and you'd better start talking fast."

Chapter Nineteen

*B*rittany refused to talk to Craig. She erased every message he left on her answering machine. He begged on all of them, pleading with her to take him back. He apologized for lying to her. He promised he wouldn't ever lie again. He said how much he missed her. He told her that he really cared about her.

"Whatever." Brittany said aloud after listening to the umpteenth message. She wasn't trying to hear it.

She was fed up with men. But, not so fed up that she didn't want to see them half-naked. She was going to check out a male review at a popular club. Some hot dancers out of Atlanta had come to town.

She didn't want to miss the show, even though she knew she'd regret it Monday morning.

Her cell phone rang and she made the mistake of answering it without checking her caller ID. She assumed that it would be April, telling her that she was on her way to pick her up.

"Brittany, it's Craig. Why won't you talk to me?" he asked in a pitiful voice.

"Craig. Damn. I already told you. You are a liar and I don't want to have anything to do with you."

"Can we at least talk in person? Can I see you again? I'm so sorry for lying to you. I was stupid."

"You're right about that. You were stupid enough to get caught. If you can lie about that, you can lie about anything. Don't call me anymore. Good bye." Click.

April arrived a few minutes later. She took one look at Brittany's face and knew that something must have happened. She sounded chirper minutes earlier when they'd spoken about the male review.

"Craig?" she guessed.

"Yeah. I answered my phone because I thought it was you. It was that dog."

"Forget him. Don't let him spoil ya mood. Let's go."

"Oh believe me. He is not going to ruin my night. I am ready to see some men take it off."

"So, where your kids at?" April asked, as she waited for Brittany to get her driver's license and club purse.

"Asleep."

April looked puzzled. "I thought you said ya sister wasn't allowed to come over here anymore. You and ya mama made up?"

"Nope. My sister isn't here. No one's here."

"You mean you don't have a baby sitter?"

"Sure don't. They're asleep and I'm going out," she said matter-of-factly.

"You gonna leave them by themselves?" April was still slightly in shock. "What if they wake up?"

"They won't."

"How can you be sure?"

"I gave them both some Benadryl. They'll be out all night."

April followed Brittany towards the door. She didn't quite agree with what Brittany was doing, but what could she do? They were Brittany's children. If Brittany thought they'd be okay alone, why argue? She had other friends who left their kids. Maybe all single parents did it at one point or another.

They went to a club called The Garage. They really
enjoyed the show, which ended up being better than Brittany
had expected. The men of First Class Entertainment turned it
out. Brittany's favorite male dancer went by the name
"Freaky," aka "Dirty Redd." April wasn't really feeling any
of them. They were too nasty. They licked on the women, let
them grope all over their private parts and even showed what
they worked with. She considered them to be whorish and
thought they probably had VD or something. No way would
she ever get involved with one of those kinky men. She had
to admit that they'd given a hell of a performance, though.
So, she couldn't hate on them at all.

After the show, the rest of the non-stripping men were
allowed into the area where the women had gathered. The DJ
played all the latest hip-hop music. The club started jumping.
April and Brittany danced the night away.

They had been dancing for quite a while when Brittany
turned around to see who had started grinding against her
butt. She stared right into the face of Craig. She sucked air
between her teeth, rolled her eyes and stalked off the dance
floor.

Craig followed her around the club all night. If she'd
wanted to meet someone else, she couldn't because he was
cock blocking.

For a while Brittany put up resistance, but in the end she
gave in. Once the club closed and everyone headed out, she
asked April if it was okay for Craig to ride home with them.

April had some reservations, but she kept her opinion to
herself. She felt that Brittany was setting herself up for
disappointment. She didn't understand why Brittany just
didn't kick Craig to the curb. She couldn't see anything
special about him anyway. He wasn't that cute and he wasn't

even fine. Maybe Brittany felt that she couldn't do any better. April just knew that Craig wasn't to be trusted. He had shifty eyes and she didn't trust men with shifty eyes. When his eyes shifted her way more than once before they all left the club, she knew for a fact that Craig was a dog. Any man who would eye his girlfriend's friend up and down all night, couldn't be trusted. But, she wasn't going to be the one to break the news to Brittany. Sometimes, it worked out best, if people found out things the hard way.

Chapter Twenty

*D*exter was still in shock. He couldn't believe that Camille had caught him at T.G.I. Friday with Meredith. Well, caught wasn't the right word, even though he was sure Camille had interpreted it that way.

Since he'd finally gotten Meredith to accept the fact that they'd be nothing more than friends, he had agreed to go to dinner with her. After his night of drinking, and morning of vomiting, he needed to put something in his stomach. They had chosen T.G.I. Friday because Meredith had suggested it.

All throughout dinner he'd talked about Camille. He'd found himself being able to open up to Meredith and tell her things that he didn't feel comfortable discussing with Walter. There was only so much that men could share. With Meredith, he could reveal his vulnerable side and not appear weak or whipped. He'd told her just how afraid he felt about losing his wife. He'd confessed that she was his best friend and the only woman that he had ever truly loved.

Meredith had listened attentively. She had let him go on and on, never once interrupting. When he'd finished, she'd gotten up from her chair, and went over and gave him a kiss on the cheek.

"What was that for?" he'd asked.

"Because you are one in a million. It's so obvious that you love your wife. Why are you even here with me? You should be with her."

"I wish I were," he'd confessed.

At that moment Camille had appeared out of nowhere. At first, he'd thought she was a figment of his imagination. But the ice in her eyes let him know that she was real.

He had introduced the two women awkwardly. Camille had glared at Meredith, not bothering to shake the hand that the other woman extended. That was not a good sign. Dexter had felt embarrassed by her behavior. He knew that the situation could prove to be volatile if he didn't do something.

"So, this is your wife that you've been speaking so fondly of," Meredith had tried to ease the tension but it hadn't worked.

"So, you two have been discussing me?" Her eyes blazed even more, if possible. "Trying to think of the right words to tell me about your affair, no doubt? Well, you can just save it, Dexter."

"Camille, please don't get yourself upset," Dexter began. "Why don't you have a seat? We can talk about this."

"I don't want to hear any of your lies," Camille interrupted. "Just go to hell." She turned and stalked off angrily.

Dexter watched as she retrieved her purse from another table. She left with two other women. Who the hell were they? He'd never seen them before. She must have met them at her new job. Had they put Camille up to confronting him in public the way she had? If so, she needed to find some more positive friends to associate with.

Dexter was concerned about his wife. They hadn't seen each other for over a week. It was just his luck for them to encounter each other under such suspicious looking circumstances. He knew things appeared to be worse than they were.

He had to talk to Camille and make her understand. It would be extremely difficult with Camille being so upset. He didn't know how to break down the wall between them but he had to try.

***

"Dexter, I am so sorry," Meredith told him after Camille had left the restaurant. "Are you alright?"

"Yeah. I just wonder if it's ever going to end." He sighed, tiredly.

"Maybe this wasn't such a good idea after all," Meredith said. "It's my fault. Dexter, don't worry about the bill. You go after your wife and make her listen. Go now."

He ended his dinner with Meredith and went back to the hotel. Once there, he began to pack up all of his belongings. He would go home and work things out with Camille. He was determined not to spend another day apart from his wife.

He arrived at home and parked his Navigator behind her Toyota Camry. When he entered the apartment he spotted Camille sitting at the kitchen table. The roses that he'd bought were scattered across the floor. Apparently, she had thrown the vase against the wall. Dexter's heart sank as he stepped over the cracked ceramic fragments and water.

"Camille, I know that you're angry with me. Can I at least explain?" he pleaded. She wouldn't even look at him.

"You were with that bitch. What is there to explain?" she asked, dully.

"Camille, it wasn't what you think."

"Well, what was it, Dexter? All I know is that my husband left me on a Friday. I don't see or hear from him for a whole week. Then, I run into him at a restaurant and he's with the woman that he swore he wasn't having an affair with. It doesn't take a college degree to figure out what's going on."

137

"There's nothing going on," Dexter insisted.

She ignored his denial. "Dexter, why did you even bother to come home? Why didn't you just stay with her?"

"I don't want her, Camille. I'm where I need to be; right here with the woman that I married."

"Dexter, last week, even last night, I would have been the happiest woman in the world, had you walked through that door and said those words to me." She looked at him with a pained expression. "But, not now. Not today. You should have stayed at the hotel or wherever you were. I don't want you near me." She got up from the table and bent down to pick up the roses that she'd destroyed.

"Camille, don't worry about that. I'll get it," he told her. He kneeled down near the broken vase.

"I can do it," she snapped, rejecting his offer of help.

"Camille please-" He reached for her hand. She coiled away from his touch. Then, without warning, her hand flew forward and she smacked him across the face.

"Don't touch me. Don't you ever touch me again," she screamed and raced from the room with tears streaming down her face.

Dexter sat there in stunned silence, holding his stinging cheek. He couldn't believe what had just taken place. His wife had actually struck him. What the hell?

Things were not supposed to be so complicated. A few months ago, he'd considered himself the happiest man in the world. Newly married, with a child on the way, overjoyed him. He had even secretly put a down payment on a four-bedroom home for when the baby arrived. He'd wanted it to be a surprise for Camille.

Now, he doubted if he and his family would ever live in that house. He wasn't even sure that he still had a family. His wife didn't trust him and he didn't know how to regain that trust. His whole world had tilted on its axis.

Dexter got up from the floor, leaving the mess. He found it hard to breathe. If he didn't leave, he might suffocate.

The last thing he needed was Meredith Walker. Running to her was not the answer. However, that's where he found himself headed. His wife didn't want him, but that didn't mean he'd be sleeping alone again.

Chapter Twenty-One

Somehow, Meredith knew that Dexter would be standing outside when the doorbell sounded. She had seen the look of fury on his wife's face when he'd introduced them. Camille had not been convinced that they weren't having an affair. Meredith doubted that she could ever be convinced. She'd known that Dexter would have a hard time trying to get through to her.

Since he now stood outside her door, she figured that things hadn't gone so well. He'd gotten rejected and had come to her for comfort.

She let him in with some reservations. She felt that Dexter had come to her on the rebound. He was hurt, confused, and who knew what else, judging by the palm print she saw on his left cheek. If she took advantage of him now, he would be sure to despise her in the morning light.

Of course she did allow herself to hold him. For a while, she could pretend. But, she couldn't pretend forever. She pushed him away with regret.

"What's wrong? I thought you wanted this?" Dexter asked.

"Well, I did, Dexter. But, after our talk earlier, I realize that it's not what I really want. Having an affair with you is not going to increase my self-esteem. Besides, if I sleep with you, you'll only regret it tomorrow."

"I won't," he denied.

"Yes, you will, Dexter. You'll be going against everything you told me earlier. So, I'll go get you a pillow and a comforter. There's the couch." She pointed.

"Okay." He threw his hands up in defeat. "You're right. I don't know what I was thinking."

"You weren't thinking. You're in pain. It's hard to think when your heart is hurting," she said softly then turned and left the room.

Chapter Twenty-Two

Camille cried for what seemed like hours. She was so confused. She didn't know what to think or how to feel. She had no real evidence of Dexter cheating. When she went over every argument they'd had, every incident, she had to admit that she had no proof.

She tried to put herself in Dexter's shoes. How would she feel if he accused her of cheating with another man, and she hadn't? What if everything that Dexter had told her was the truth? If that were the case, then the finger would point back to her as the cause of their marriage ending.

She thought about the finality of that statement. Was their marriage really ending? It definitely wouldn't last if they kept going the way they were headed.

She felt a jolt in her heart when she thought about life without Dexter. If he left her forever, she didn't know how she'd be able to handle it. Despite their problems, she loved him with her whole being.

Shame washed over her as she laid in bed, staring into the darkness. She had slapped her husband. How could she have ever done something so cruel? No matter what he'd done, violence had no justification. How could she hurt him like that? Two wrongs did not make a right.

She wanted desperately for things to change between them. She longed to feel her husband's arms around her. She ached for him. That longing and aching made her get up and go seek him out.

When she peered into the living room, she found an empty couch. It was after midnight and her husband was gone. Only this time, it might be for good. She had finally managed to push him away. Well, if he hadn't cheated with Meredith before, she couldn't guarantee that he wouldn't go to her now. Why wouldn't he? She, herself, had opened up the door and shoved him out with her distrust.

She went back to bed and just lay there. She prayed fervently that Dexter would come back home. She needed him. She was finally ready to talk. They'd resolve everything. It wasn't too late.

Hours passed but Dexter didn't return. She called his cell, but it went directly to voice mail. Camille cried and prayed. She got up and paced the floor. She cried some more

"Damn. Damn. Damn," she sobbed as she stared at her wedding picture. She picked it up and traced Dexter's face with her index finger. "I just gave you to her, didn't I?" The light in her eyes turned dull. She fell to her knees.

When morning arrived, she was curled up on the bathroom floor, with her face pressed against the cool tile. All of the crying she'd done had managed to make her sick. She didn't have the energy to pick herself up and get back in the bed. If she had lost her husband, she didn't think she could handle it.

Chapter Twenty-Three

Dexter stretched out his arms and legs and turned onto his back. Meredith's couch was smaller than the one at his house. Even though it wasn't leather, it still wasn't all that comfortable. He sat up and yawned loudly.

"Well, good morning," Meredith's voice called from the kitchen. She had heard him stir and peered around the doorway.

"Good morning," he mumbled. He was sort of embarrassed by his behavior from the night before. He hoped Meredith wouldn't hold it against him.

"Do you want breakfast? I usually don't eat. I drink a Slim Fast, but I can fix you something quick," she told him. "How about some scramble eggs and toast?"

"Naw. Don't go through any trouble because of me. I'd better get home." He rubbed the sleep out of his eyes. "I know Camille is probably sick out of her mind with worry," he said quietly.

"So, will you be in to work today?" Meredith asked, stepping into the room.

In three years, Dexter had never missed a day of work without scheduling it in advance. Well, there was a first time for everything. He didn't think he could conduct business as usual, feeling the way that he did.

"No. I think it would be best for me to take the day off, considering." He had slept in his clothes and they had gotten wrinkled. He pulled on his shoes and stood up.

"I'll let Bill know," she told him.

"Thank you." He reached for his keys on the glass coffee table. "Hopefully, I can clear things up. If not—" He let the words trail off into the air.

"Everything will be fine. Just take one day at a time," Meredith advised.

"I guess that's all I can do. Well-" He sighed loudly. "I'd better head out. Thank you for making me take the couch." She understood all that he didn't say. She just nodded.

"You're welcome." Meredith watched as he walked towards the door. He turned, smiled sadly, and left.

She went back into the kitchen to get a Slim Fast out of the refrigerator. She heard the doorbell and thought that maybe Dexter had left something. She hurried to answer.

"Dexter, did you fo-" Her words trailed off. It wasn't Mr. Gray as she had assumed. Meredith was shocked to find his wife standing there. She took a step back.

Camille had fought down her morning sickness, determined to confront Meredith Walker. She knew that the time had come to meet the harlot who her husband had turned to. He'd probably spent the night with her, too.

Thinking that she'd catch them in the act and have the evidence that she needed, she hadn't bothered to get dressed. She'd thrown on a thick terrry cloth robe and house shoes, hurrying to her car.

Now, she stood eyeing the other woman. She kept thinking how badly she wanted to fuck the bitch up. She tried to remain calm as she glared at the tramp standing in front of her. Up close she didn't look anything like Vanessa Williams Fox. Her forehead was too big and her hazel eyes were clearly Acuvue. Fake bitch. She was probably wearing a hair weave. It took everything within Camille's power to prevent her from grabbing a handful of it. She wanted to snatch it out and give it back to the horse it had been taken from.

"Where is my husband?" Camille demanded. Her eyes were bloodshot and her hair disheveled. She had a dangerous look in her eyes that Meredith couldn't quite decipher.

"I don't know," she managed to get out. She was very much unnerved. Never had she expected to be confronted in such a manner. Dexter had told her that his wife was a sweet, even-tempered, loving woman. So, who was the rude person bombarding her doorstep, a clone?

"You're a damned liar." Camille pushed past her and entered the living room.

"You have no right," Meredith told her. "Whether he's your husband or not, you have no right barging into my house. Now, get out before I call the police," she warned.

"Call the fucking police, bitch," Camille snarled. "You don't know who you're dealing with. I don't give a damn about the popo. Now, are you going to tell me where my husband is, or do I have to tear this whole fucking house apart?"

Meredith was at a loss as to what to do. She had concluded that Mrs. Gray wasn't in her right frame of mind. She didn't want to upset her any further. There was no telling what the crazed woman might do.

"He was here," she finally admitted. "But, he left a few minutes before you arrived."

"So, I was right all along. You've been fucking my husband?" She glared at her, disgusted.

"I haven't. I swear," Meredith denied, vehemently. "He slept on the couch," she added. "Mrs. Gray, Dexter doesn't want me. He loves you. He left and headed for home in hopes that he could work things out between the two of you."

Camille looked around the room. She seemed to contemplate whether or not to believe Meredith. Finally, she saw the rumbled comforter on the couch. She stared at it for a moment. She walked over to the couch and picked it up. It held Dexter's familiar scent. She replaced it and turned to Meredith.

"Well, maybe you didn't sleep with him. But, let me give you some friendly advice." Her eyes bore into Meredith's. "You should be more careful in the future. You never know when someone's a loose cannon. You may end up getting yourself cut," she threatened. She opened her robe and that's when Meredith saw the butcher knife. "Think about that, the next time you decide to go after someone's husband. I could have been some psychotic bitch who'd hurt your trifling ass." She walked away and slammed the front door so hard it amazed Meredith the glass panes didn't shatter.

Meredith dropped the can of Slim Fast she held because her hand shook so badly. She slipped to the carpeted floor and cried hysterically. She thought about calling the police but dismissed it. She had brought everything on herself. When you make your bed, it's inevitable that you have to lie in it.

Chapter Twenty-Four

Brittany snuggled up closer to Craig's warm body. They had made love for hours the night before and had just finished that morning. She had thought that he would never stop. He was like a machine and she couldn't get enough of him.

He had put her in one sexual position after the next. He'd tossed her and turned her, massaged and caressed her from head to toe. He'd licked, nipped and bit her. He'd done just about everything. The response that he received from her increased his desire. Finally, she was completely worn out and begged him to stop. He chuckled knowingly and rolled off. He had fallen asleep shortly after and she'd curled up next to him. She felt like a fat cat basking in the sun. She wanted to purr; she felt so good.

To hell with work, she thought. She reached for the phone and called in with a lie about being sick. They would have to make do without her. She wanted to spend the day with her man. She'd decided that she could forgive him for lying about not having any children. As long as he didn't lie to her about anything else, everything would be cool.

She got up and went into the bathroom to take a shower. She saw Craig's wallet by the sink. It took her only a moment to make a decision. Surely, he wouldn't have anything else to hide from her. After all, they had cleared the air. He'd promised her he had changed.

She opened it and looked through the different compartments. Finding nothing suspicious, she started to close it. On impulse, she looked where he kept his money. Folded up behind all of the bills, she found a letter of some kind. She pulled it from the wallet and laid the wallet to the side.

She unfolded it. For a moment, she thought that he'd won an award or something for recognition on his job. The paper was a copy of a certificate. It wasn't until she read the words on the paper, that she got the official message.

It was a "Coochie Coupon" from someone named Coca. Whoever Coca was, she had taken the time to get on a computer and make up a coupon. It informed Craig that he had a free invitation to get some "coochie" anytime, anywhere, whenever he wanted it.

Brittany turned red hot with fury. How in the hell could he carry something like that around in his wallet, when she was supposed to be his woman? Did he plan to cash in his "coochie coupon?" How many had he already cashed in on?

She had let him off easy the first time he'd lied. He would not get off the hook with this one. It was time for confrontation. She stalked back into the bedroom.

"Craig. Craig. Wake up." She shook him roughly.

"Huh?" He stirred a bit then turned over on his side.

"Get up. I have a bone to pick with you."

"What?" He asked groggily, rubbing the sleep from his eyes.

"You need to go throw some water on your face because I want you to be completely alert for this."

"What are you talking about? Can I get some sleep? You wore me out," he told her, reaching for the cover. Brittany snatched the sheet and pulled it off the bed.

"I said get up. I want you to explain this "coochie coupon" to me." She said firmly.

Craig's eyes popped open and he sat up.

"What?"

"This." She held it up in front of his face. "What exactly does it mean?" He squinted at the document then he chuckled.

"Aw girl, that ain't nothing. Just something from my ex-girlfriend."

"Why is it in your wallet?" she questioned.

"It's been there for months. I just never took it out. I didn't really think about it. Now, can I get some rest? You know I have to go to work."

"That's all you have to say? You don't think there's anything wrong with you having a free coochie coupon in your possession from your ex-girlfriend, when you're with me?"

"What's the big deal?" he asked.

"The big deal is that I want you to get up and get out of here. You're nothing but a liar and a cheat. If this has been there for months, why does the date on it say September 7th? That was last week," she pointed out.

Craig had gotten caught, but of course he didn't admit to anything. He knew that Brittany was mad, but she'd calm down eventually. He'd let her have her way and leave. He'd act like he was remorseful and call her later to apologize. It always worked. He was sure it would work again.

"You're tripping about nothing. You're always looking for the worse in me. When are you going to learn to trust somebody?" He tried reverse psychology.

"I trust you as far as I can throw you. Now, leave.'

"Alright. I thought after last night that you and I could have something special. You're the woman that I want to be with. That coupon don't mean nothing. Why are you doing this, Brittany? You gonna let something so lame break us apart?"

"Get out." She refused to give in to him. She was beginning to feel that Craig had no respect for women. He was also a habitual liar.

"Okay. I'm going." He stared at her with sad eyes. "I'm sorry," he offered.

She balled the piece of paper up and threw it at him.

"Go to hell."

Craig picked it up. Hell, he may need to use that. It seemed like Brittany would be pissed off at him for a while. Maybe he could convince Cocoa to give him some. After all, she had given him the coupon. He closed the door but not before he saw the look of fury on Brittany's face.

She'd get over it. And if she didn't, oh well. He was too heartless to give it much thought, one way or another.

Brittany watched Craig get into a burgundy Toyota Camry with some thin, anorexic looking chick. She had refused to drive him home or let him wait inside her apartment. She didn't even want to look into his sorry face. After she'd allowed him to call someone to come pick him up, she'd insisted that he wait outside.

Maybe Cocoa had come for him. She had a mind to go outside and tell her what type of man Craig really was. But, she was too tired and disgusted to even care.

Let him go. If he stayed in her life, she might end up in the Pinellas County Jail. Then again, he just might wind up six feet under.

Brittany had puffy, red eyes because she'd cried all day long. She didn't want to leave the house, but she had to pick up her children. She forced herself to get up and put on some clothes. She still had over an hour before it was time to get her youngest child, so she flopped down on the couch in front of the television. It was on some soap opera; one that she wasn't familiar with. She did recognize one of the actors, Shemar Moore, because she watched Soul Train and he hosted the show.

She let her mind go back over the events of that morning. She couldn't believe how callous Craig had treated her. He didn't care about anyone but himself. He was such a jerk. Why did she always pick the wrong type of man?

She thought back on her growing up years. Her mother and father had separated when she was very young, so she'd never really had a father figure around to depend on. Her mother had always been too busy to offer her any guidance or advice about anything, let alone boys. Consequently, she'd had her first sexual experience at the age of twelve. She didn't know anything about precautions or birth control pills. She was just a child. When she became pregnant shortly after she turned thirteen, it was no surprise.

Of course, it shocked her mother. She couldn't believe that Brittany would bring such shame upon the family. They were Jehovah Witnesses. Something like that happening was definitely frowned upon. After the initial shame wore off, her mother began to give her too much attention. She became a virtual prisoner in her own home.

She wasn't allowed to go anywhere or do anything without her mother's consent.

After she'd given birth, her son was hers to take care of. Her mother was not the one to baby-sit, so that she could run in the streets.

There would be none of that. She had to care for her child and go back to school. She didn't have a life outside of baby diapers, homework and the Kingdom Hall. In the midst of it all, she did graduate from high school.

At age sixteen she'd met Todd. His family practiced as Jehovah Witnesses also. Both families threw them together. By seventeen, she had gotten married and headed to another state to begin her life as Todd's wife.

Marriage to Todd was not a bed or roses. Todd, for one, was irresponsible. He didn't help with any of the housework. He paid the bills late all the time. He rarely came home. When he did, he either ignored her or told her how much she disappointed him.

Brittany stuck it out for two years, the unhappiest years of her life. When she found out that Todd cheated on her, she'd decided to call it quits. Even though she was nine months pregnant with her second child, she got on a plane headed for home.

Of course her mother thought that she had made a huge mistake. All men cheated. It was in their genes. You just dealt with it and moved on. She argued with Brittany, telling her that she couldn't get on a plane in her condition. She should just forgive Todd, and stay with him until the baby was born.

When Brittany found out that she couldn't fly in her advanced state of pregnancy without a doctor's note, she got on the computer and forged one. She had been determined to leave Todd. She didn't want to wait until after the baby came. She wanted nothing to change her mind. So, with the fake documentation, she flew home. Thirty minutes after she landed at the Tampa International Airport, she went into labor. Her mother complained all the way to the hospital.

Brittany couldn't understand why she couldn't find someone decent. Over and over, she kept hooking up with the same type of low life. Craig topped them all. He actually believed his lies.

Brittany's phone rang, breaking her out of her reverie. She checked the caller ID because she'd didn't want to chance picking it up and hearing Craig's voice. It was an unknown number. Judging from the area code, the person calling was out of town. Her curiosity got the best of her and she answered.

"Hello?"

"Can I speak to Brittany Anderson?" an unfamiliar voice inquired.

"Speaking."

"My name is Jessica Butler and I want to know why I found your number in my man's pants' pocket?"

Brittany was momentarily speechless. "W-who is your man?" she finally asked.

"Craig Booker. Craig. Do you know him?" the other girl asked.

"Well, before today, he was supposed to be my boyfriend," Brittany told her.

"How long have you two been together? He and I have been together for two years. The only thing is that I'm in Tallahassee attending college. So, we only see each other every other weekend."

"Oh really?" A light went on inside her brain. Now she understood clearly. "Craig told me that he was in the Army Reserves."

That was his explanation for being away two weekends out of a month."

"Army Reserves? He can't get in the Army. He has a felony charge on his record for assaulting his baby mama. The Army wouldn't take his sorry ass."

The two talked for a while longer. Brittany told her about Cocoa and her coochie coupon. Jessica told her that she didn't want to have anything more to do with Craig.

"Well, neither do I. If he's lying to you, me and some ho named Cocoa, there's no telling who else he's screwing around with," Jessica informed. "Girl, if I was you, I'd go get myself checked out. I know I am. Apparently, Craig is a straight up dog. He just might have the mange, if you know what I mean."

Brittany felt so depressed after her conversation with Craig's girlfriend. After that morning, she thought there would be no more shocking revelations. She realized that she didn't know Craig at all. How could she be so wrong about someone?

She remembered everything she'd done for him. She'd driven her car to Brandon countless number of times to pick him up because his car was a piece of crap. She'd dyed his nappy ass hair every three weeks because he was prematurely gray. She'd also helped him get the job where he currently worked by typing up an impressive resume. She'd even made sure that he'd gotten to the interview on time. That meant she got up at five in the morning and drove to Brandon, so that he could make it to his eight o'clock interview. Needless to say, she had arrived late at her own job. Hell, she'd even sucked his limp dick and licked his hairy ass balls. There was no telling how many other mouths and lips had done the same thing.

She felt physically ill thinking about all the things she had done in bed with Craig. She prayed that he hadn't given her any sexually transmitted diseases. If she could hurt him and get away with it, she would. Inside her, the anger festered.

Chapter Twenty-Five

When April finally made it to work at ten o'clock, she saw that Brittany wasn't at her cubicle. She also noticed that Camille's desk was empty. She got an odd feeling in the pit of her stomach.

Brittany might show up late or could possible call in because of Craig. She still didn't know what Brittany saw in him. Camille was probably stressing over catching her husband with that woman at T.G.I. Friday. She hoped that everything would turn out okay for her girls. She made a mental note to call Brittany on her first break to find out what had happened.

April could feel eyes boring into her and gazed up. It was her manager. She was so tired of her. She knew that the woman meant well, and was just doing her job, but hell. Sometimes, she took her job entirely too seriously. April wished she'd just stay off her ass.

Of course she got called into the office. Only this time, it wasn't the regular office. She had to go to the back room. She knew that meant trouble. When something serious transpired, employees got escorted to the back room, the room without a view. April, prayed that she still had a job.

April felt a migraine begin at her temples. It had started as just a regular headache but had graduated by mid-day. She had taken two Ibuprofen pills and two more Tylenol capsules about an hour and a half later, yet it still hadn't subsided.

She didn't know if partying Sunday night, lack of sleep, or stress brought it on. Maybe it was a combination of all three.

Of course she had received a written warning from her manager, Angie, for being tardy to work again. She was placed on R I (Requires Improvement) status. That meant she would be on probation for three months. So, for three months she wouldn't be able to receive any recognition, any bonuses, or pay increases.

April felt disappointed, being that she was one of the top processors. If she wasn't going to get any incentives, she wasn't going to continue to bust her ass typing. She'd slack just like everyone on RI status did.

Plus, she had counted on getting a raise in October. Now that she wasn't going to get it, she was upset. She'd fallen two months behind on her car payment. She found herself paying a late fee for rent every month. It depressed her. That's why she drank so much and went out clubbing frequently. It was her way of coping with it all.

On top of everything else, she received a call from her daughter's school. Peaches had complaints that her stomach ached and the school had insisted that April pick her up. That only added to her stress because she had to face her manager again to ask if she could leave.

Of course, Angie had thought she'd made it up. April had to give her the number to the school so she could call and confirm that her daughter needed to be picked up. That pissed April off. She really felt that Angie disliked her because she was biracial. She always felt as if she was being analyzed when they'd had meetings. Maybe Angie should have become a shrink instead of a supervisor in the medical billings department.

She called Brittany on her break and found out that she had gone through some more drama with Craig. That figured. April wasn't the type to say, "I told you so," but it did cross her mind. She promised to stop by later so they could talk.

She headed to Pinellas Park. Peaches' school had to be way out in the boondocks. She damn sure didn't feel like driving out there, but she had to get her daughter.

It took about thirty minutes to get to the school. When she went to the office, Peaches was waiting, sitting in one of those orange chairs swinging her feet back and forth. She had a pout on her face.

April ignored the look and signed her out. They left the office. Peaches drug her feet as she walked behind her mother.

"What took you so long?" Peaches complained. "I was waiting forever and ever," she exaggerated.

"Shut up and just get in the damn car," April yelled. She didn't feel like going through it with Peaches. Her head pounded.

"My stomach hurts," Peaches whined.

"Shut up about it. Get in the car. We're going home. What the hell else can I do about it?"

"I wish you'd stop yelling at me. All you ever do is yell," Peaches complained, getting into the back seat. April slammed the door.

"So fucking what? I'm the damn adult. I can yell when I fucking feel like it." April slammed her own door and started the car. "Now, shut ya damn mouth."

"You need to stop yelling. Don't raise your voice, raise your child." She heard from the back seat. For a moment she thought about turning around and whacking Peaches a good one, but she didn't.

"Alexis." She was so upset that she'd resulted to using her daughter's real name, which she didn't do often. "I don't want to hear another word out of you. I mean it. If you say one more thing, I'll drop you off at ya Grandma's house and leave you there for the rest of the week," she threatened.

"Whatever." Peaches said and turned her body sideways. She crossed her arms and stared, sulking, out the window the rest of the drive home.

April didn't know what to do with her oldest child. The girl had a smart-aleck mouth and was all "attitude." She was hardheaded and rarely listened to anything she instructed her to do.

She thought long and hard on the drive home. Alexis's father had hinted around about picking her up and letting her spend the weekend with him. He had two other daughters that were close to Alexis's age that he kept every other weekend. April decided that it was time to start getting along with him. She needed all the help she could get with her daughter. It would be good for Alexis to get to know her father as well as her sisters.

She exhaled as she stopped at a red light. When she arrived home, she would make an important phone call.

Chapter Twenty-Six

Dexter didn't see Camille's car in the garage so he figured she'd gone to work. He pulled his Navigator in and got ready to close the garage door when Camille pulled up. He left the door open and waited for her to get out of her car. When she did, he stared at her strangely. She wore only a housecoat and slippers. Her hair was wild. If he didn't know his wife, he would have thought that she was some random, mad woman. Obviously, she wasn't dressed for work.

"Where have you been looking like that?" he asked. He almost laughed until he saw the anger flash in her eyes.

"I went to pay your girlfriend a visit and to offer her a little friendly advice," she said, stalking past him and into the house. He hurried behind her.

"No," he groaned. "Please tell me you didn't." Dexter couldn't believe Camille would resort to that. "Meredith had nothing to do with any of this. It was all on me."

"Well, it's too late to try and protect her now. You might find yourself looking for a new secretary soon. I don't think she'll be sticking around much longer."

"What did you do?" he demanded to know.

"What I had to do, since you wouldn't do anything." She removed the knife from the pocket of her robe and slammed it on the kitchen table. Dexter's eyes widened as he stared at the weapon. "I gave her a lot to think about," Camille snarled.

"You went over there and threatened her with a knife? Are you out of your mind?" He stared at her incredulously.

"Maybe I am," she said curtly.

160

"This is not a game. You can't just go around threatening someone. What if she'd called the cops? Aggravated assault is a felony. What the hell were you thinking?" he yelled.

"Don't stand there shifting the blame to me. You're the one who fucked up. You shouldn't have taken your ass over there in the first place."

He glared at her. At that moment he hardly recognized her. Was this the woman that he'd married?

"I don't even know who you are anymore," he finally said.

"I'm the same woman that you said, "I do," to four months ago," she reminded him.

He shook his head from side to side. "I don't think so. I have never seen this side of you. You have lost all control. You need to get yourself together."

Hearing that made something inside Camille snap. "No, you need to get your shit and leave," she hissed, pointing toward the door.

Dexter stood there in silence. It seemed like an eternity before he answered. "I hope that you're sure that's what you want. If I leave this time, it's because you put me out. You can't blame Meredith. You can't blame your damn hormones. All you can blame is yourself." He approached her and stared down into her face. "If I leave, I won't be coming back. I'm not your damned yo-yo, Camille. So, is that what you really want?"

Camille held his gaze. She felt so much anger and confusion. What was wrong with her? Was she really going over the edge? Why was she refusing to bend a little? All she had to do was make an effort to meet Dexter halfway. They could work their problems out. They had to try.

She turned away. She didn't want him to see the pain in her eyes, the doubt, and the insecurity.

"No," she said quietly. "No, I don't want you to leave," she told him. "I want things back the way they used to be. Am I asking for too much?" Her slender shoulders shook as she cried and it moved Dexter. He couldn't stand to see his wife in so much pain.

"No," he answered. "No, you're not asking for too much." He sighed. "But you can't keep letting your emotions rule you. You have to learn to control your outbursts. The last thing you need is to be sent to jail. It will be a miracle if Meredith doesn't decide to press charges against you. I can't believe that this has gotten so out of hand."

Now that she had calmed down, she could think about the seriousness of what she had done. She really had gone overboard. Now she could relate to all those people that had been declared temporarily insane.

She gently massaged her temples, feeling the beginning of a headache. Suddenly, she felt lightheaded and nauseous.

"How are we going to resolve things, Camille?" she vaguely heard Dexter ask. "We can't keep going like this." Dark spots appeared behind her eyelids. She felt herself fainting and reached out to break the fall. She thought about the baby as the darkness engulfed her.

Camille awoke and found herself in bed. She remembered what had happened and immediately reached down to touch her stomach. She breathed a sigh of relief. Her baby was still in there. He or she was safe. She vowed never again to do something as irresponsible as she'd done earlier. Confronting Meredith could have had an adverse affect. What if Meredith had attacked her? She considered herself lucky that no harm had come to her unborn child.

Dexter peered into the room. He saw that Camille had awakened so he entered.

"You gave me quite a scare, Mama," he said quietly, taking a seat next to her on the bed.

"I'm sorry. Sorry for everything," she said with great remorse.

"Well, now is not the time to discuss this. You need your rest. The paramedic who attended to you, told me to make sure you remain in bed- at least for the next two days."

"But- my job-" she protested.

"Don't even worry about that. That's minor. I'll call them and explain. If they can't understand, you don't need them. I earn more than enough money to provide for you."

"But I got the job in the first place in order to help you out. I don't want you struggling to pay for everything," she said.

Dexter gazed at her with affection in his eyes. This was the woman that he'd fallen in love with, a caring, compassionate person. This was the Camille that he knew.

"Baby," he said gently, taking her hand in his. "I don't mind taking care of you. And it's not a problem at all. I don't have any financial struggles. As a matter of fact, I recently put a down payment on a four bedroom house in Lakewood Estates," he said.

Camille's eyes widened with surprise. "Did you really? Dexter, we're buying a house?" she asked excitedly.

"Yes. Now calm down. I don't want you getting too excited, now." He squeezed her hand. "I want us to have a home. I want us to be a real family. Promise me, no more acting all crazy on me. Okay?"

"I promise," she said gently. "I am so sorry for being so jealous."

"Like I said, we'll discuss everything later. For now, you need to rest." He leaned over and kissed her gently on the forehead. "I'll be back a little later to check on you. Get some sleep."

"Thank you."

"See you." He walked out and closed the door quietly.

Camille closed her eyes. She couldn't believe that they were going to move into their own home. Lakewood Estates was a very prominent, predominately Black neighborhood populated with gorgeous homes. One of those sports stars lived out there. She tried to recall his name—Gary Schofield or something to that effect. She knew she'd love living there and couldn't wait to see their new house. She fell asleep dreaming of white picket fences.

Dexter called Camille's supervisor at the employment agency. He explained why she couldn't make it in that day and also requested that she be off for the rest of the week. The woman understood and seemed sympathetic. She'd wished her a speedy recovery.

He didn't really know how to apologize to Meredith, but he knew he should try. He called the office, but she wasn't there. Bill answered the phone, wanting to know what was going on. Dexter appreciated the fact that he didn't try to pry. He assured Bill that he'd handle the situation and explain everything later.

He dialed Meredith's home number. He wasn't surprised when she didn't answer. He was worried about her, but his first concern went to his wife. There was no way that he would run off and leave Camille when they'd finally made some progress.

Dexter felt optimistic about the future. He knew that they had a long way to go and by no means would they win the "couple of the year" award, but at least they were communicating.

He went into the kitchen and fixed a grilled cheese sandwich and a bowl of Campbell's soup. He placed it on a tray and took it to his wife.

When he walked into the room Camille was leaning over the side of the bed, holding her stomach. Dexter's heart leapt to his throat.

"What's wrong?"

"I don't know. I went to the bathroom and there's blood," she told him.

"You mean you're spotting, right?"

"I don't think that's it. There's so much blood. Something's wrong. I think I'm losing the baby." Her voice held fear. "Dexter, what are we going to do?"

He dropped the tray of food down and rushed over to her. "I'm taking you to the emergency room." He picked her up and hurried from the room.

Dexter had been sitting in the waiting area for what seemed like an eternity before a doctor appeared. He was feeling anxious and on edge, worried about Camille and the baby.

"Mr. Gray?" The doctor was short, blonde, and rather young. His nametag read Michael Harris.

"Yes. I'm Mr. Gray." Dexter got up from the hard, plastic chair that he'd been sitting in. "Is my wife okay?"

"She's fine," Mr. Harris told him in a hushed tone. "However, she did lose the fetus," he added.

"No," Dexter moaned. It felt like a vice gripped his heart upon hearing the news.

"I'm terribly sorry. Unfortunately, the fetus had been dead for quite some time. It expelled itself from the womb. There was nothing that we could do." The doctor delivered the news in a professional manner. "Your wife is resting. But, you can go see her now." His brown eyes held compassion.

"Thank you," Dexter said mechanically. Through a haze, he watched the doctor walk off.

His baby couldn't be dead. He felt at a loss as to what to do. It was his fault. He blamed himself. Maybe if he hadn't left, Camille wouldn't have lost their baby.

Now, he stood outside her hospital room. He wanted to go in and offer her support, but he couldn't. He kept thinking about the role he had played in the loss of their child. He didn't know if he'd ever be able to face his wife again.

His hand touched the doorknob, but he let it drop. What if Camille couldn't forgive him? What if she hated him? He couldn't handle that right now.

He put his hands in his pants pockets, turned and walked away. Doctors, nurses, and other hospital personnel passed him in the hallway. He was oblivious. Numbness consumed him as he left his wife lying alone in her hospital bed.

It devastated Camille when she found out that she'd lost the baby. She felt as if her heart had broken into a thousand pieces. She knew that her baby was gone; she just couldn't accept the truth.

She stared at the door of her hospital room, dreading the moment when Dexter would walk in. She didn't want to see the accusing look in his eyes. It was her fault that their baby had died. She didn't know if he'd ever be able to forgive her. She couldn't even forgive herself.

She thought about those times when she'd wished her pregnancy away. The guilt tore away at her. She accepted the responsibility for her own pain. She couldn't stop the hot, scalding tears that filled her eyes. She wanted her baby. She desperately needed Dexter to hold her and tell her that it would be okay. But, he never came and she grieved alone.

Chapter Twenty-Seven

April sat in Brittany's living room and listened to her soap opera like drama about Craig. They drank strawberry daiquiris, while the children played in the boys' room.

"So, who is Cocoa?" April asked.

"He claims that she's his ex-girlfriend. I don't know. But I'm going to find out." She got up and went to pour another drink. "I should be a private investigator. I have a way of finding things out."

"Well, maybe you should just leave it alone," she suggested. "Just forget about him. He ain't even worth it."

"Nope. I can't let him off the hook so easily. He's got to get paid back for what he's done."

"You're talking crazy. Just forget him," April advised.

"No, he needs to be taught a lesson," Brittany insisted. "Just like I taught Jarvis a lesson."

"Who?"

"That idiot that I told you about a few months ago. Remember, he had the girlfriend but had lied about it?"

"Oh yeah. What did you do to him?"

"Set him up. He wanted to keep seeing me and her so I arranged it. I invited her over."

"No."

"Sure did. When he walked in and saw her, the look on his face was priceless."

"What happened?"

"She beat him up right in my living room."

"Damn."

"He won't be playing games with anyone else no time soon."

"Okay. You do what you feel is necessary. But if you end up in jail, don't be calling me to bail ya ass out," April told her.

April wondered if Brittany had lost it. She'd heard of women doing crazy things; like slashing car tires, breaking windows, and other insane stuff. She didn't now what Brittany was capable of because she was hurting and didn't want to admit it. Craig had done a number on her.

April got up and poured herself another drink. She realized that her headache had resided. She didn't need Tylenol or Bayer; a drink provided the necessary medicine she needed. Everything would be just fine.

Brittany's phone rang.

"Turn the music down." she instructed, picking up the receiver. "I can't hear." April got up and turned the volume knob on the stereo. "What? This is Camille?" Brittany listened for a few minutes then hung up.

"What's going on?" April wanted to know. She could tell that it was something drastic from the look on Brittany's face.

"That was Camille. She's in the hospital," Brittany informed. "She had a miscarriage," she ended.

"Aw man. Well, should we go down there?"

"No, we can't. Visiting hours are over for today. She said that they're going to release her tomorrow morning. So, we'll go see her at home."

"Well, at least she has her husband."

"Yeah." Brittany went to the kitchen and poured her drink down the drain. "That does it. I don't feel like drinking anymore."

April finished the rest of her daiquiri. She felt there was no sense in wasting good liquor. She couldn't do anything about Camille's loss, except feel sympathy for her. That was all anyone could do.

Chapter Twenty-Eight

When Dexter picked her up from the hospital they said very little to each other. He helped her into the car and drove home with few words. She couldn't really read him because he wore dark shades.

She wondered what he thought about. Did he blame her? Was his heart breaking, too? All of these questions played tag inside her head. She didn't pose any of them to her husband, though. The arrived at the house and she'd been shut off in the bedroom ever since.

Silence filled the room. No television. No music from the stereo, just total silence. Also, complete darkness.

That's the way Camille wanted it. She had told Dexter that she didn't care to see anyone- that included Brittany and April. She couldn't consider anyone else's feelings just yet; she was the one in pain.

As she lay in the darkness, she thought back over the last four months; from the time she'd met Dexter in the department store where she worked, to the day they'd walked down the aisle.

She remembered being so happy on her wedding day. All of her family had attended, as well as Dexter's adoptive family. She had thought that nothing could go wrong.

She had looked simply radiant in her white gown with the long tail trailing behind. She'd beamed as she went down the aisle and stood next to Dexter. They had both exhibited so much affection and love on that special day.

Unfortunately, that happiness hadn't lasted. Once the morning sickness set in and her hormones went whack,

Dexter had started working later and later. She had started to feel neglected and it made her angry. It hadn't taken long for her to develop feelings of insecurity and jealously.

When Dexter took Meredith Walker out to lunch, that fact alone had been enough to set Camille off. She didn't want her husband hanging out with a woman like that, even if she did work with him.

After all, Meredith had a gorgeous, slim body. Meanwhile, she continued to get fat and unattractive. At least, her mind had her thinking so.

She had to admit that she had pushed Dexter further and further away with her suspicions and accusations. What man would stick around when all she did was look for evidence of his guilt? In her eye, he had been guilty until proven innocent.

Now, the miscarriage had driven her and Dexter even further apart. She felt entirely responsible for losing their child. She couldn't do anything to bring the baby back. She felt such emptiness inside. She doubted that the void in her heart could ever be filled.

The doctor had prescribed sleeping pills for her. He'd told her that they'd help her get through the first few sleepless nights. She took one of the pills and turned onto her side.

By habit, she reached down to rub her stomach. She felt nothing but the flatness of her abdomen. The pain in her heart was excruciating when it hit.

Her baby was dead. She'd need more than just sleeping pills to get her through the days to come.

Dexter sat in the living room, not that Camille even noticed. He did everything he could to keep his mind occupied. For the most part, he played the PlayStation. From

the time he arrived home from work to the time he went to
bed, he sat in front of the video game.

He remembered all the arguments that had occurred
because he hadn't been home when Camille felt he needed to
be. Now, he was around, but she'd shut herself away in the
dark. She could care less about him, or anything else for that
matter.

On the few occasions when he had tried to talk to her, she
didn't respond. She'd just stare at the ceiling or the wall;
whichever one she was looking at during the time he entered
the room.

She didn't want anything to eat. She wouldn't answer the
phone and she didn't want visitors. She'd told him repeatedly
that she wanted to be left alone, so he had finally complied.

Now, he'd grown sick of video games. He might as well
have gone to the sports bar. It was Friday night and he sat at
home holding a damn joystick.

He unhooked the video game and turned on the TV.
Wrestling played on the channel. He watched The Rock for a
few minutes and then picked up the phone and tried
Meredith's number.

He had been unsuccessful in reaching her all week. He
wanted to express how genuinely sorry he was for his wife's
behavior.

It momentarily threw him when a male's voice answered.

"Hello? May I speak to Meredith Walker?" he asked,
composing himself quickly.

"Who the hell is this?" the guy bellowed.

"Dexter. Dexter Gray. I'm her boss," he added. Whoever
the guy was, he sounded pretty uptight. Dexter didn't want to
get Meredith into any trouble if it could be avoided.

"Just a second," the other man told him in a more civil tone. Moments later, Meredith got on the line.

"Hello?"

"Hi, Meredith. It's Dexter. I was worried about you," he began. "I've tried to reach you a few times, but all I got was your machine. Are you okay?"

"Yes. I'm fine," she said rather evasively.

"Are you sure? I know that what my wife did must have shaken you up. I want to apologize for that."

"Okay. Well, I can't really talk right now," she told him.

"Okay," he said, puzzled. Meredith sounded rather strange. "Who answered your phone?" he asked, out of curiosity.

"E- er, that was Brandon."

"Brandon?" Dexter was taken aback. "Isn't that your ex-boyfriend? The one who abused you? Meredith, what's going on?" he demanded.

"Mr. Gray, I really can't talk about it. I know I've been out for the past week, but I'll be back on Monday," she said suddenly.

"So, you still want the job?" he asked. "I mean, due to the circumstances, I wouldn't blame you if you resigned."

"I'm not going to quit." Meredith paused in their conversation. Dexter heard Brandon's voice in the background. "Yes, that's right, Mr. Gray. Monday. I'll be in to work first thing Monday morning. Thank you, Mr. Gray. Goodbye." The click of the phone disconnecting sounded in his ear as she hung up on him.

Well, he wouldn't have to worry about Meredith making any advances towards him anymore. If she and Brandon had gotten back together, he doubted she'd have the courage to speak to him or even glance his way.

Dexter went back to watching wrestling. He decided to do something that he hadn't done in a while; have a cold beer. He got up and went to the refrigerator.

Soon, he forgot about Camille hiding out in the darkness. He forgot about the pain he felt due to losing a part of him. He forgot about Meredith. He forgot everything.

It wasn't long before he fell asleep on the couch. One beer had turned into two, and so forth and so on. He'd emptied the entire six-pack of Budweiser. The crushed cans lay on the floor next to him.

Chapter Twenty-Nine

Another Saturday found Brittany still seething inside from being conned by Craig. She'd sat around for the majority of the day, trying to think of ways to make him pay. Finally, she'd decided to gather up all of his clothes and other personal items, and pour bleach on them. However, doing that didn't give her the satisfaction that she craved. She wanted to do something more. She wanted to hurt his doggish ass.

She called April to see if she wanted to ride with her to Brandon. "I'm going to take Craig's stuff to him. I don't want anything more to do with him," she explained. April agreed to go along, so fifteen minutes later they drove down I-275 headed toward Brandon.

"So, when you give him his shit, that's going to be the end, right?" April asked.

"Yeah, I don't want to ever see that dog again. I can't believe that he was lying to me the whole time. There's no telling how many women he had, stringing them along."

"Well, he'll get what he deserves," April pointed out.

"Yeah, maybe sooner than he thinks," Brittany said through clenched teeth.

"I don't like the sound of that," April said half jokingly, half seriously. "I hope you don't plan to do nothing crazy."

"Who? Me? Would I do that?" Brittany laughed a hollow, bitter sound in April's ear. She began to regret that she'd agreed to come along. She didn't want to be a part of anything that could become criminal. She wasn't in the mood to go to jail. Craig and Brittany's problems should be theirs. She wished she had never involved herself, but she couldn't turn around.

For the remainder of the trip, they traveled in silence. Brittany seemed to be deep in thought. April prayed that Brittany wouldn't do anything to Craig that could lead to her arrest. It was all a big mess.

Finally, they arrived at their destination.

"How do you know that he's here?" April asked as they sat in the car.

Brittany had pulled up next to a big, older model, car.

"That's his raggedly ass car," she said. April stared at the heap of metal. It was in bad shape. It had peeling paint. Rust covered it and the front fender was gone. April couldn't believe that Brittany dated a man with a car in such a condition. That sign along should have warned her that he'd be trifling and no good.

"I found out from his sister that this is where he really lives. Of course, he lied about living with his mama, too. He lied about everything." As she spoke, she got angrier. She reached into the back seat and grabbed the basket filled with his clothes. "I'll be right back," she told April, getting out of the car.

"Hey, are you sure you should go to his place? What if his girlfriend's there? She might be crazy. What if she tries something?"

"I wish she would," was the reply. "The way I'm feeling, I'll fuck her ass up."

April sighed and got out, too. She'd have to go along with Brittany. She wasn't going to just sit in the car and chance something happening to her friend. She slammed the door of the passenger's side.

"Damn. Why did I have to come?" she cursed as she followed Brittany. By the time she got up the stairs, Brittany was banging on the door of what April assumed to be Craig's apartment. No one answered.

"Craig. It's Brittany. I know you're in there, you chicken-hearted bastard. Why don't you come out and face me, you coward," she yelled. She pounded some more. The door finally cracked and an eye peered out.

"Brittany, stop tripping. You're loud. I don't want everybody around here in my business. Calm down," he said through the crack.

"Calm down my ass. So, where is your girlfriend? Is she hiding behind you? Why don't you let her come out so that we can introduce ourselves? Scared of what else we might discover about you?"

"Stop it, Brittany. Now, I know you're mad, but you ain't got to be acting like this. We can talk about this and work it out."

"I don't want to work nothing out with you. You are a lying dog. I just came to bring you back all of your stuff. Here it is." She took the basket of clothes and other personal items of his and turned it upside down. Everything flew over the second-story balcony. April watched in horror as shoes, socks, underwear and other accessories flew in the air. Everything was bleached and faded. She tried not to laugh. She didn't want to encourage Brittany any further, but it was comical.

"Brittany. What did you do that for? Now, you know you're wrong."

Craig finally came outside. He raced down the stairs to where his belongings were scattered about on the concrete. He began to pick things up. "Damn." He realized that

Brittany had bleached and ruined everything. "Brittany." He threw up his hands. "You have lost your mind. These clothes cost a lot of money," he yelled up to her.

"Of course they cost a lot of money because I bought them. Since I paid for them, I can do whatever I want to them."

"You're crazy."

"I'll show you crazy." Brittany flew down the stairs. April thought for sure that she would attack Craig, but she didn't. Instead, she got in her car and started it. When she accelerated and headed straight for Craig, April knew that her friend had gone over the edge.

"Oh shit," Craig yelled and began to run. He leapt onto the hood of his car. Brittany continued to drive. She didn't stop like April thought she would. She rammed the front bumper of her Honda into the driver's side of Craig's car. She backed up and rammed it again.

"Now, that ought to teach you not to play games with people," Brittany yelled, getting out of the car and heading for Craig.

April's heart pounded a mile a minute. She rushed over and pulled Brittany by the arm.

"Girl, what the hell are you doing? You want to go to jail? Let's get the fuck out of here before someone calls the police," she suggested.

"I wish I had crushed his slimy ass in the ground," Brittany hissed. "I'm going to fuck him up."

"No you're not, Brittany. We have to go now." April tried to restrain Brittany, but she was livid. They ended up getting into a scuffle in the parking lot. Finally, April gave Brittany a slap that brought her back to her senses.

"Stop fighting me and let's just go," April told her. "That nigga is not worth spending time in jail."

Huffing and puffing Brittany got back into the car. She sat with a tight grip on the steering wheel, glaring at Craig who stood at a safe distance on the other side of his car.

"Brittany, snap out of it. Let's get out of here before we both end up in jail." The panic in April's voice finally got through to her. She backed out of the parking space and sped off, leaving black tire marks on the asphalt.

It amazed April that they made it back to St. Petersburg without being pulled over by any cops. She glanced through the rearview mirror, expecting to see flashing lights and hear sirens. When they finally pulled into Brittany's driveway, April breathed a sigh of relief.

"I'm never going to go anywhere else with you," April threw at Brittany.

"Girl, I'm sorry for how I acted back there. I just lost it," Brittany apologized. "I just wanted to hurt that bastard."

"It's all good. Let's just forget about it." April followed her into the house. "Well, I hope that's the end of it. If you take him back after this, then you really are crazy."

"I wouldn't take that dog back if he was the last dick on earth," Brittany mumbled.

April just nodded. She knew that Brittany believed what she'd said. She was still wound up. But, after everything had calmed down, and Craig started sweet-talking her again, April didn't know how Brittany would react. She knew of a lot of women that went through similar situations ended up going back to the men who'd done them wrong. It's like they thought they deserved it or something.

April prayed that she would never be that desperate or lonely or whatever. She just wished that Brittany would meet someone else and move on. Craig was not worth the pain.

"Now that you're single again, let's go out tonight. Maybe you'll meet a new man," April suggested.

"Yeah, but he'll probably be a dog. They're all dogs," she said dully, plopping down on the couch. "I'm never going to date again. I'm going to turn gay," she stated.

"Girl, you are really tripping. You ain't turning gay. You like dick too much," April said.

"You had one, you've had them all. I'm going to turn gay. I mean it. Men are such liars and cheats. They're all the same," Brittany insisted.

"Well, that's just the way it is. You just have to learn to beat them at their own game. Get them before they get you," April pointed out. "I guess I'm the one to talk, right? I'm single. I just don't have time for the drama. Besides, any time I meet somebody and try to start something, my baby daddy comes back and messes things up."

"Just like a man. Selfish dog," Brittany snarled. "He doesn't want you, but he doesn't want anyone else to have you. He wants you to always be available for him when he wants a piece of ass."

"Well, he ain't getting no more of this ass, here. It's over and I mean it. After that last time, I will never let him use me again."

"We all say that. We've been through so much bullshit, over and over. But, we still keep letting it happen. What does that say about us?" April shrugged. "I mean, we're not stupid. We're attractive, fine, somewhat together financially. Why can't we find some decent men? Are we cursed?" Brittany asked.

"I hope not. If so, I'm going back to that spiritual healer and get me some more candles. Maybe that'll help."

Brittany stared at April with an incredulous look on her face. "You went to a spiritual healer? You don't even believe in God," she reminded.

"Yes, I do. I just don't go to church," April argued. "Those candles are good luck. I'm going to get some more."

"Forget the candles. Let's go to the XXX store and get some vibrators," Brittany suggested.

"That's a good idea. At least a vibrator is always hard, unlike most of the men I know."

"Yeah, plus it can't lie to you, because it don't have a mouth," Brittany cracked.

"Some of them have tongues, though," April revealed.

"Really?" Brittany's curiosity was peaked. "Like a real tongue? Does it work?"

"Hell, I don't know. I don't have a vibrator," April told her.

"Maybe that's our problem. Maybe we both need to get one."

They had a male bashing session and swore off men, then decided to visit an adult store to see what they could find. No more men meant no more sex. They had to find a bedroom replacement in order to survive the dry spell.

April, who'd visited the store a few times, wasn't nearly as excited as Brittany. She'd seen the different vibrators, motion lotions, sex toys, whips, masks, handcuffs, lingerie, etc. She'd even bought a few items and had put them to good use. However, she could use a vibrator because for now she wasn't getting any action. She would never sleep with Darren again and she'd slowed down on picking up strange men in the club since the last incident. She needed something to get her through the lonely nights.

"Where's that tongue thing you mentioned?" Brittany whispered, walking up one aisle and down another, fascinated.

"It's over there with the vibrators. Hey, check these out," she held out a pair of Ben-Wah Balls.

"What are those for?" Brittany asked, taking them from her and looking at the package.

"It's something the Japanese use. They're supposed to vibrate."

"You put them where?" Brittany asked, staring at the small balls.

"You know, in- your- stuff," she emphasized.

"I don't know about that. What if one gets stuck up in there? I would be too embarrassed to go to the emergency room." They roared with laughter. April took them and placed them back on the shelf.

"Girl, you are crazy."

"Hey, this is cute. It's pink," Brittany pointed out.

"Well, that's because it's called the Lil' Pink Kit." She looked closer. "It is cute," April agreed.

"It has a pink mini vibe, pink crystal love beads, and little pink feather," Brittany read from the box.

"What's a jelly ring?" April asked.

"I think that's for the male to use." They stared at the kit in fascination. "I'm getting this. It even has some cherry lube."

"Sounds tasty. I'll get one too. I can think of some things to do with that pink feather."

"Girl, you're nicety: nice and nasty." They cracked up again as they looked around the store at other items.

Teresa D. Patterson

In the end Brittany chose a pair of Velcro, furry handcuffs, the pink kit with accessories, some different flavored motion lotions, and a red sheer negligee with matching thongs. April just got the pink kit.

That's the only thing you're buying?" Brittany questioned when they reached the front counter with their purchases.

"Yeah, because I already have most of those items on a top shelf inside my closet," April joked.

"You undercover freak."

"A woman's gotta do what a woman's gotta do."

They left the adult store with their purchases, talking excitedly. For the time being, Brittany forgot about Craig.

Even after she'd hit his car and bleached his clothes, Craig kept calling. Brittany remained adamant in her decision to not see him anymore. But, he continued to call her so many times. Finally, she got so tired of hearing his voice she call-blocked him.

She had to admit, he'd really had her going. She had been sprung. When she spent time with Craig, she floated on cloud nine. He was her one true, soul mate. He had even gotten close to her children. She'd had to break their hearts by telling them Craig would no longer be coming around.

His lies and deception had really hurt because he'd pulled the wool over her eyes. She couldn't believe that one phone call had shattered her happiness. The call she'd received from Jessica Butler had been the icing on the cake.

She probably would have forgiven him for having the coochie coupon in his possessions. That wasn't solid proof that he'd been unfaithful. But, she couldn't forgive him for actually cheating.

184

A week had passed since she'd rammed his car, but she was far from being over him. She had fallen hard. No matter how he'd wronged her, she felt in her heart that he really loved her. That's the reason she didn't slam the door shut in his face when he showed up at her apartment.

"What do you want?" she barked. She tried to remain cruel and uncaring.

"Can I come inside? I really miss you and I'd like a chance to explain everything. Since you won't talk to me on the phone, I didn't know any other way except to come over. Will you at least hear me out?"

Brittany wanted to stay angry because had had hurt her so badly. She couldn't build a wall around her heart even if she wanted to.

Craig was a smooth operator. He knew how to break down all of her defenses. He talked his way back into her life and into her bedroom.

They made wild, passion-filled love for hours. Craig had Brittany climbing the walls and calling out his name. Once she'd reached orgasm for the third time, she made up her mind- she didn't care who else he'd slept with- Craig belonged to her.

They fell asleep exhausted, but satisfied. Brittany assumed Craig would spend the night, but he woke up around midnight and began pulling on his clothes.

"Where are you going?" she asked groggily. She rolled over and threw her legs around his waist.

"I have my cousin's car and I have to get it back to him," he told her. "I wish I could stay." He playfully slapped her on her healthy backside. "I'd love to get up in that again," he said regretfully. "But, I can't." He finished dressing and stood up.

"When will be the next time I see you?" she questioned. The suspicion lurked in the back of her mind.

"I'll be back tomorrow, baby. I promise." He leaned over and kissed her. She slipped her tongue into his mouth and they played tongue tag for a minute.

"Stop that now, you gonna get me started again," he warned.

"That's my intention."

"I know, but I have to get going."

"Okay," she sighed. "You want me to walk you to the door?"

"Naw, I'm good. You just get some sleep. I'll let myself out."

Craig left and the cloud of doubt settled over her like a thick fog.

He had lied once, why should she believe that he wouldn't do it again? He'd proven to be a master at manipulation and deception, but she still couldn't resist him.

Brittany tossed and turned, trying to shake the doubts. She finally fell into a troubled sleep.

It wasn't long before Craig went back to doing slime. It seemed that he wasn't nearly as concerned about being caught since Brittany had already taken him back twice.

Brittany had purchased him a pager and it vibrated all night long. He received one page after the next. Women. Each a different number. Brittany found out about them all because she called the numbers. She'd even figured out his code and accessed his voice messages.

One woman after the next confirmed that she had or was currently sleeping with Craig. None of them seemed to care that he was supposed to be her man. One had even had the

audacity to reveal she knew about Brittany and had even had
sex in her bed. She claimed that Brittany had been at work
and Craig invited her over for a mid-day rendezvous. The
trick had the nerve to laugh at Brittany and call her stupid.
She ended the conversation by telling Brittany she'd rode
around in her car, too. That irked the hell out of her. Not only
had the heifer ridden her dick, she'd ridden around in her car.

Every woman that she contacted sounded like trifling,
trashy, whores. Brittany wondered if Craig had used
protection with all of them. She knew that he didn't like to
wear condoms. He'd said they were "too small" for him.
She'd purchased Magnums and he'd begun using them. After
a while, they'd resorted back to doing it naturally, because
he'd sworn he wasn't sleeping with anyone but her.

She thought about all those skanks and all the times she'd
gone down on him. She might as well become a lesbian since
she'd munched carpet anyway, in a sense.

Craig's lying, scheming and cheating had finally caught
up to him. Through all the women and their confessions,
Brittany found out who his real girlfriend was. Her name was
Carmen.

Carmen called Brittany to plead with her to leave Craig
alone. She cried and carried on, accusing Brittany of breaking
them up. According to her, they'd lived together for four
years and planned to get married. Carmen believed things
between herself and Craig would be fine if Brittany exited the
picture.

Brittany had assured the disillusioned girl that she wanted
nothing to do with Craig. She had recommended that Carmen
cut him loose too. But Carmen had insisted that Craig loved
her and she felt the same.

"Well, good luck," Brittany told her. "You definitely will need it."

After her final breakup with Craig she became buck wild. She hung out every night that she could find an open club. Sometimes she went with April, other times, she'd go alone. More often than not she met someone. She usually ended up following the guy home or they'd go to her place. If he proved to be good in bed, she'd continue to have a sexual relationship, if not, he got dumped. The next week there'd be someone else. Brittany didn't care. She felt empty inside and didn't know how to fill the void. She felt worthless, unlovable and used up. She knew that some of the men she'd slept with in the past had dogged her out.

She'd heard all the mean comments they'd made. She was known as being "off the chain" or the latest, "Got too many miles on that motor- need a new engine." Her self-esteem slipped to and all-time low, but she convinced herself that she was just fine.

Chapter Thirty

Camille awoke from her drug-induced sleep. She felt groggy. For a minute, she couldn't remember anything. Then, it rushed her in a flood of pain. She wasn't pregnant anymore. Her baby was gone.

She felt so hollow. She had nothing. She didn't want to go on feeling such raw pain. Her baby had died. Her marriage was over. She had nothing to live for.

She reached for the bottle of sleeping pills on the nightstand. She wondered what would happen if she took five or six of them. Hell, why not the whole damned bottle? Nothing mattered anymore.

She tried to swallow more than one pill but gagged. She needed water. She glanced over at the glass and saw that it was empty. She picked it up.

It took all of her strength to drag her tired body out of the bed and to the bathroom. She filled the glass with water and went back to bed.

She sat on the edge, contemplating what she was about to do. Would it be the answer? She wasn't sure. She just knew that she had to stop the hurt, somehow.

Before she could talk herself out of it, she snatched up the bottle of pills, emptied the contents into her palm and tossed them into her mouth. She swallowed them down with the water. She nearly choked with the pills all going down her throat at once. Finally, it was done.

She had managed to swallow all of them. She lay back on the bed. For a moment, she thought about Dexter. She wondered what he'd think when he found her lifeless body, whenever he decided to check on her.

She almost regretted her decision to take her own life. Her husband would be devastated. He'd already lost his unborn child, what would losing his wife do to him? Camille tried to picture Dexter's face as he stared at her body in a casket. It jolted her back to her senses.

Her heart pounded in her chest and she began to panic. It suddenly occurred to her that she didn't want to die. She had made a huge mistake. What could she have been thinking? She got up from the bed and made her way into the living room. Where was Dexter?

For days, Dexter had remained home. He didn't leave the house. He'd check on her every other hour, but now that she needed him, he was gone. Damn. She felt herself growing weaker. The pills had begun to take an effect on her. She knew that she only had a matter of time before she succumbed. She reached for the phone and hit the redial button. She had no idea who Dexter had called last. She just knew that in her state, she couldn't see the numbers on the phone to dial anything.

"Hello?" The voice sounded familiar, but Camille couldn't recall where she'd heard it. "Hello? Is this Dexter?" the person asked.

"H-hello?" Camille said weakly.

"Who's there? Is this Mrs. Gray? Camille?"

"I- don't know where Dexter is," Camille began. Suddenly, she felt desperate. She didn't want to die. "I need help. I took a bottle of sleeping pills. I need help. I don't know where Dexter is," she said again, now frantic.

"Oh my God. You just hang on, okay? I'm on my way over there. Just stay on the phone. Can you understand me? Stay on the phone. Talk to me."

"Okay." Camille gripped the phone tightly. What the hell had possessed her to take those pills? The last thing she wanted was to cause Dexter more pain. If he found her dead, that's exactly what would happen. How could she be so selfish? How could she hurt the man that she loved yet again?

In her haze, she now realized how unfairly she'd treated Dexter. Day in and day out, she had accused him of being unfaithful. No wonder he didn't want to be around her. At that most crucial moment, she realized her mistake. She loved her husband. She prayed for a chance to be able to tell him. She wanted to let him know just how sorry she was for all the accusations she'd hurled his way.

"Hello? Are you there? Camille, are you still on the line?" She finally recognized the voice on the other end of the phone: Meredith Walker. Wasn't it ironic that the woman she'd threatened to kill would be the one who would end up saving her life?

Chapter Thirty-One

*M*eredith had transferred her home phone to her cell. She drove around thinking about all that had happened. She wanted to put some space between herself and Brandon. A week before, he'd just shown up on her doorstep, swearing that he had changed. She wanted so desperately to believe him, but she should have known that a leopard never changed his spots. Brandon had proven to be the same abusive jerk that he'd always been, when he'd twisted her arm that morning.

Instead of backing down from Brandon, she'd taken a stand. She'd snatched her arm from his grasp and slapped him across the face, hard.

"Don't you ever put your damn hands on me again," she'd warned. "Don't think that I'm going to take that shit from you ever again. I don't deserve your abuse, Brandon. No one does." She'd told him to his stunned face. "Now, I'm going out for a while and when I return, I expect for you to be gone. You and all of your belongings," she added. She turned her back and walked out.

When her phone rang, she had expected Brandon, calling to threaten her or to beg for forgiveness. When she'd heard the desperate voice on the other end, it had alarmed her.

She drove down 31st Street South, breaking the speed limit, to get to the other woman. She couldn't let her die. She didn't know why Camille had chosen to call her, but that was irrelevant. She would do her best to help her.

192

She'd told her that she'd taken some sleeping pills. Maybe she hadn't taken a fatal dosage. Meredith prayed that she could just get there in time.

"Camille, are you still there?" she spoke into the phone.

"Yes," Camille replied. "I'm so tired. I want to go to sleep."

"No," Meredith screamed into the headset. "No, don't do that. I'm pulling up to your place right now. I'll be right there." Meredith hurriedly parked her car and jumped out running.

Thank God the door was unlocked. Meredith let herself in. She saw Camille leaning against the doorframe, trying desperately to stand. She raced over to her.

"Do you know how many pills you took?"

"I- I dunno," Camille slurred. "Maybe six, eight, t-t-ten."

"Come on. I got you." Meredith led her to the bathroom. She'd heard somewhere that cold water would keep the person awake. Her main concern was that Camille would fall asleep and never awaken. She couldn't let that happen.

She shoved the other woman into the tub and turned on the showerhead full blast. Camille spluttered and gasped.

"Cold."

"I know, but it's necessary." As she struggled to hold Camille up with one arm, she dialed Dexter's cell phone with her free hand. She breathed a sigh of relief when he answered.

"Hello?"

"Dexter, this is Meredith. You need to come home immediately. Your wife needs you. It's an emergency." She didn't have time to explain. She needed both hands to hold Camille up because she was slipping, so she dropped her cell phone. She prayed that Dexter would get there soon.

It wasn't long before God answered her prayers.

"Camille." Dexter's voice boomed through the apartment.

"In here, Dexter. Hurry," Meredith called out.

"What the hell is going on?" Dexter asked as soon as he saw Meredith holding his wife under water. Was she trying to drown her or something? He didn't know what to think.

"Your wife called me," Meredith explained, seeing the shock on Dexter's face. "She took some sleeping pills. I'm trying to keep her awake."

"Aw, naw. Sleeping pills? God." Dexter's voice cracked with emotion. "Is she okay?"

"Well, she's still awake. Do you think I should call 911?" she asked in concern. "She said she took about six."

"No, no, no." They heard Camille mumble.

"She needs to get those pills out of her system," Meredith told Dexter. "Do you have something that can make her vomit?"

"I'll be right back." He rushed from the room and returned with a bottle of cod liver oil. He helped hold his wife until she drank a large amount.

"Ugg," Camille groaned. "Nasty. I'm going to throw up."

"Good, that's the plan," Dexter said. He took her from the shower and led her to the toilet. He held her up as she hurled the cod liver oil and pills back up.

"That's it. Just get it all out," Dexter crooned. "I know it hurts, but let it all come out."

"You think she's going to be okay?" Meredith had stood in silence, watching as Dexter tended to his wife. Dexter nodded. "I'm going to get her something dry to put on. Start taking those wet clothes off of her, okay?" Dexter nodded again and began doing what Meredith instructed.

"God, Camille. Why would you do such a thing?" he asked in anguish. "Don't you know that you are the most important part of my life? Without you, I am nothing. Do you understand that? If I lost you, I don't know what I'd do." He pulled her into his arms, sobbing.

Camille realized just how deeply her husband loved her. Maybe he didn't say it as often as she liked, but his actions proved it. It broke her heart to hear him crying. She reached up and held his face in her hands.

"Dexter, I am so sorry," she said, staring into his eyes. "I love you. I will never hurt you again," she told him. "I promise."

"I love you, too. Don't ever forget that." He kissed her. The kiss held love, compassion, promise and hope for the future. Camille didn't want to let go of her husband. She finally knew without a doubt that he did, indeed, love her.

"Now, let's get you into something dry," he said.

Chapter Thirty-Two

Brittany became determined to forget about the past and move on with her life. She hadn't run into Craig at the clubs she frequented. If she did, there would be no telling what she'd do. She still had the desire to hurt him and didn't know when it would subside.

She called April to see if she wanted to visit another club in Ybor City. April agreed and volunteered to drive. Brittany went to shower and get dressed. That night, she anticipated seeing the available men on the prowl. Even though she didn't have a babysitter, she'd made up her mind that she was going out, regardless. If she stayed home, she'd only end up depressed, sitting around thinking about Craig. Besides, her kids had fallen asleep before April arrived to pick her up. What would it hurt if she left them for a few hours? They wouldn't even know she was gone.

They arrived just as the crowd was picking up. April went to the bar for drinks and Brittany stared at the people on the dance floor. She had brought her purse into the club because she didn't want to carry her cell phone around and chance leaving it someplace. She felt the phone vibrate at the bottom of her purse and dug it out.

Figuring the caller was one of her many male friends, she glanced down at the caller ID. Her heart jumped into her throat when she saw her own home phone number.

"Hello?" Her voice was anxious when she answered.

"Mama, you have to come home. There was a fire." Her eight-year old son said in alarm.

"Where is your brother?" she asked in fear.

"He's here with me. We're going next door to the neighbors. There's a fire truck at our house," he said, excitedly, not knowing any better.

"I'm on my way," she yelled. Rushing over to April, she grabbed her arm. "I have to go home," she said with desperation in her voice.

"What's going on?"

"My house caught on fire, or something. I don't know. I have to get to my kids."

"Well, come on." They ran from the club.

It seemed to take an eternity for them to arrive back at the house. In actuality, it only took about fifteen minutes since April drove 85 miles per hour. Brittany felt full of dread. She had put her children's lives in jeopardy, just so that she could have a good time. How many times had April warned her not to leave the kids at home alone? How many times had she ignored her conscious? It took this drastic act to make her realize just how precious her children were to her.

How would she explain things to her mother if something happened to her kids while she went out to party? How could she explain it to anyone? There was no excuse. All of these thoughts ran through her head. She began to cry silently.

When they got to the house Brittany learned that the extent of damage was minor. A candle that she'd left burning in her bedroom had fallen over onto the bed. The mattress had a gigantic hole in it and the room was covered in soot, but that was it. It all could be replaced or repaired.

However, her problems were far from being over. The police on the scene had called Children and Family Services when they'd realized the children were unsupervised. They informed her they would be taking the children into custody until they'd had an opportunity to investigate further.

"What do you mean, you're taking my kids?" Brittany asked in disbelief.

"Ma'am, don't you know it's against the law to leave your children unattended?" A uniformed officer questioned. "You're lucky that you're not going to jail." He frowned at her distastefully and walked off, mumbling something about young, irresponsible parents.

"When am I getting them back?" she asked.

"That's entirely up to you," she was told. "You'll have to go through the necessary steps to prove that you're a fit parent," the on-call social worker informed.

"I am a fit parent," Brittany argued.

"Going to the club and leaving your kids alone doesn't prove that," the lady said, sarcastically, smirking at Brittany's club clothes. Brittany couldn't deny that she'd been out partying. It was written all over her face.

"I was only gone for a short period of time."

"And that's all the time it takes," she said, not giving Brittany any slack.

"What am I going to do without my kids?" Brittany asked, when it finally registered that her kids would be taken away from her that night.

"You should have thought about that before you left them alone." The social worker had no pity. She'd seen so many similar cases that it disgusted her. When would young parents ever learn? They were living in a selfish, callous society. Didn't they know that their children should always come first? She shoved a card into Brittany's hands. "Call the office tomorrow. You'll find out what you'll need to do in order to get your children back," she said coldly, and walked away.

Brittany was devastated. How could this have happened? She wasn't the only mother in the world who'd left her kids in the house alone. Why did they have to take her kids? It wasn't fair.

She couldn't do anything except stare at her two boys with tears streaming down her face as they sat in the back of the social worker's car. She felt so powerless. The guilt ate away at her.

The next day, Brittany sat in her mother's living room crying for hours. She was inconsolable. Her mother had tried to offer her advice and words of comfort, but nothing got through. Finally, her mother just put a blanket over her and left her alone.

The situation forced Brittany to reflect back on her life. She had started having sex at an early age when she didn't really know what sex was about. She just did it because she wanted the boys to like her.

She knew nothing about the emotional consequences that came along with being intimate. No one had told her. Since she'd started so early, she hadn't given herself a chance to experience true intimacy.

It had all been a game to the men who'd had her. Now, there were so many of them that all the faces just ran together. Before Craig stepped into her life, she'd gone through one man after the next. It had become a pattern. She felt that no man really wanted her. All they wanted was what she could give them sexually.

It all stemmed from her upbringing. She'd felt so unlovable that she had gone looking for love anywhere she could find it. She remembered running away from home on several occasions because her mother had beaten her. Those were the times that she'd experimented with sex, not really caring about what happened to her. She had just wanted to feel loved.

She could also remember all those times that her mother had left her and her three siblings alone in the house. But, unlike Brittany, her mother hadn't given them the run of the house. They'd been dead bolted in one room. All of the windows had been sealed, with no chance of them getting out. The phone had been locked up. They had been all alone. When she'd tried to tell someone about the abuse, they'd shushed her up. They'd told her that she was making things up and she should be ashamed of herself. Her mother worked hard to raise four children on her own. She shouldn't be so ungrateful. She should be proud to have such a caring mother.

Right.

Now it seemed that she wasn't so different from her mother after all. Even though she had tried so hard not to ever be anything like that woman, she'd turned out to be just like her. What was that saying? The apple doesn't fall too far from the tree. It was true. Just like her mother had neglected them, she had neglected her own children. It was all the same. She now had to suffer the consequences for her actions.

Was it really worth it? Did she really have to go out and party and leave her children alone? Did she need to run off in the middle of the night to see whatever man had decided to call her and hook up with him and leave her kids? She also recalled all the different men that had stepped in and out of her life. What kind of an example could she set? How would her boys grow into men who knew how to respect women if they looked toward her for guidance?

What was wrong with her? Didn't she love her children? Had her mother ever loved them? These were questions that she didn't really have all of the answers to. She didn't know why she did some of the things that she did. She just knew that she couldn't live without her children. If she'd ever felt empty in her life, at this moment, she felt the most emptiness. No man, no amount of alcohol, or partying could fill the void in her heart. Only the love of her two sons could do that.

She had to get them back. She would do everything in her power to prove that she could be a decent parent.

She found the card that the social worker had given her the night before. With trembling fingers, she picked up the phone and dialed the number.

"I'll do whatever it takes," she said aloud "-whatever it takes to get my kids back."

Unknown to Brittany, her mother stood a few feet away. She knew that Brittany struggled to hold on to her sanity. It had to be so hard to do under the circumstances. Watching her daughter go through so much pain broke her heart. God knew she'd experienced so much in such a short time. Mrs. Woods knew that what had happened to Brittany was partially her fault. It was learned behavior. If it was all you knew when you were growing up, it was only natural that you ended up doing the same things.

She'd just gotten to the point where she could admit she'd made an awful parent. She had married too young and had children too fast.

She'd felt smothered because of all the responsibilities once her husband had left. Going out and partying was an outlet. At the time, she didn't think about the children and how it would affect them. All she'd cared about was her own selfish needs.

Now, as she stood looking at her daughter, she realized the damage she had done. The daughter would have to pay for her mother's sins. There was no getting away from it.

The guilt she felt was so great. If only there was a way to turn back the hands of times. If she could do it all over again, she'd do things so differently.

The last thing she wanted was to lose her grandchildren forever. She loved those boys. Somehow, she thought that she could make up for some of the pain she'd caused her daughter, by giving her grandchildren all of the love and affection that she couldn't provide for her own children. Apparently, it hadn't worked.

She ached inside. She couldn't imagine what her daughter felt. If it was anything like the pain that she was feeling herself, then she was truly sorry for her.

Chapter Thirty-Three

*T*he events of the night before really shook April up. She tried to call Camille but got her answering service. She felt so badly for Brittany. She couldn't believe that Children and Family Services had actually taken her children. It came as a shock. It made her realize that she was no different than her friend. Those could have been her children. How many times had she just gone to the store and left her own children in the apartment? Plus, she had to admit that she'd done the same thing that Brittany had done when she couldn't get her mother to baby-sit just the week before. She'd left them alone and had gone out on a date. Thankfully, nothing had happened to them.

April felt such a depression settle over her. She couldn't imagine how it all had affected Brittany. Her heart went out to her.

As she thought about Brittany's situation, she heard a knock. In her vulnerable state, she forgot to answer her door with the security chain in place. When she saw her son's father standing there, she couldn't speak. She hadn't seen Darren in a while. The main reason for that was because she had avoided him. Now he stood there looking upset.

"Why you been keeping me son from me?" He started in on her immediately.

"I haven't," she denied. "I've just been busy."

"Yeah. Whatever," he snapped. He walked into the apartment before she could shut the door in his face. "You're just trying to be nasty."

"I'm not. I told you, I've been busy."

"You must got yaself a man. You tripping bad," he snarled.

"Darren, you need to go. I am not in the mood to argue with you," she said tiredly.

"You know what? You ain't nothing but a bitch," Darren exploded. He glared at her with disgust. "You're a sorry excuse for a mother. You think you can keep my son from me, well, you better think again. I can take better care of him than you can." He stared at her, waiting for her reaction.

"You ain't even got a job," she told him. "What the hell can you do?" she retorted, getting angry. She didn't know what to make of him coming in her house, disrespecting her and thinking nothing of it.

"So what? So, you got a job? It don't matter. You always hollering that you broke. You can't never pay ya bills. You ain't never got no money. You don't buy him nothing. You'd rather be at the mall trying to buy an outfit for the muthafucking club. You don't care nothing about him." His voice was raised and his face contorted. She had never seen him so angry and filled with hatred.

"I think yo' ass betta leave. You said what the fuck you had to say, so you can go now." She opened the door, leaving him no other option but to walk through it.

"I don't give a fuck about what you do," he said stiffly, pointing in her face. "You just need to stop trying to keep my son away from me. If you wanna run around here being a trick, that's your choice. But, I will see my son." He glared at her angrily, and walked out the front door. Before she could close it, he grabbed it and slammed it shut. "Trifling ho," he yelled.

"Fuck you," she yelled back at him through the closed wood.

Her heart constricted with pain. She couldn't believe that Darren would say such hurtful things. He was her son's father. How could he stand there and say those things about her to her face? It hurt. It hurt like hell.

What love she'd had for him dissipated in that instant. Even though they'd gone their separate ways, she'd always hung on to the hope that they'd find their way together again. That dream would never become a reality. She almost hated Darren. She couldn't imagine ever wanting to be with him again. He'd finally voiced his true opinion of her and that opinion had hurt her to the core. She couldn't help herself. She sat on the couch, put her head in her hands and just cried.

Chapter Thirty-Four

Camille sat wrapped in a thick cotton robe. Meredith brewed some Maxwell House coffee and poured a cup for each of them. Finally, they all sat, ready to discuss everything that had happened.

Meredith hadn't wanted to impose on Dexter and Camille when she'd overheard their conversation in the bathroom. She had felt like a third wheel. She'd done what she'd come to do and was going to slip out of the apartment quietly, when Camille called her.

She entered the bathroom, hesitantly.

"Meredith, I want to thank you for everything," Camille told her quietly. "I owe you my life," she said.

"I'll don't know how we'll ever be able to repay you for saving my wife's life," Dexter added. "Thank you. You didn't have to do what you did."

Meredith didn't know what to say. She handed Dexter the robe that she'd retrieved from the other room. Camille shivered.

"You really should get those wet clothes off. I'll go make a pot of coffee and then we can talk," she'd told them.

Now, they all sat sipping from their cups of steaming coffee.

"Like I said before," Dexter started, "I want to thank you for saving my wife's life. I don't know why you did it, but I'm glad you found it in your heart to help her."

"Especially after what I did," Camille joined in. "I want you to know that I am so sorry for threatening you like that. I was out of line. I had no right. For a minute, I think I lost my mind. I honestly believe that I went temporarily insane." She stared down at her hands that were clasped together in her lap. "I mean, who in their right mind would do something like that?" She asked no one in particular. "And then, the pills…" Her voice trailed off. She got choked up. "I am so sorry. I'm sorry for everything- for accusing you of having an affair with my husband and for threatening you."

"I understand. You've been under a great deal of stress," Meredith said. "I know that I didn't make the situation any better. I could just sit back and pretend that I had no part in this, but that would only be a façade. I'm guilty of being attracted to your husband," she admitted and glanced at Dexter. "I came on to him. I flirted shamelessly. I even went so far as to throw myself at him." She shook her head in self-disgust and sighed deeply. "But, Dexter didn't want any part of it." Now, her gaze rested on Camille as she spoke. "He didn't want me. He told me from the beginning that he was not interested because he loved you," she told Camille truthfully. "So, I'm the one who should apologize to you, to both of you. I had no business trying to interfere with a marriage. For that, I am truly sorry."

The three of them talked for a while longer. Camille decided not to tell anyone about her episode. She didn't want people to know about her mental break down. Some people could be so judgmental. They wouldn't understand and if she got medical personnel involved, they'd make more out of it than what was necessary. They'd probably go as far as having her admitted to a mental facility for observation.

If that happened, she'd always be labeled. She didn't want that. Living life was already difficult enough.

Meredith vowed that she would respect Camille's wishes and not tell anyone. Camille had the right to make that choice and she understood. One of the hairstylists who worked at her beauty salon had been labeled "crazy." It had followed her for the majority of her life. The woman had even believed that she was indeed, "crazy," for many years. She'd taken the prescribed medications and had even lived off a monthly check because of her mental inability to work. Now, she was one of the most popular hairstylists in the city and would be opening her own salon in a few months. She had decided that she wasn't crazy after all and had wanted more from life than an SSI check each month. Meredith guessed it was all about self-esteem and how you perceived yourself. She was glad that Camille could understand her actions. She didn't need any stigma following her for the rest of her life.

After giving Camille a hug and wishing her the best, she left. She arrived home to find that Brandon had taken all of his belongings and left. He was nowhere to be found. It was the perfect ending to a not so good start.

* * *

Camille got up to get the empty coffee cups.

"Don't worry about that, babe. I'll take care of it," Dexter told her. "After all you've been through I think you need to relax."

"No, that's the last thing I need," Camille told him. "What I need is for my husband to make love to me."

"Do you think that's a good idea?" Dexter questioned. "I mean, you just had a miscarriage."

"Dexter, if it wasn't okay, I wouldn't want to do it. I just know that right now, I'm very fertile," she said.

"Are you saying what I think you're saying?" Dexter asked. "You want to try to have another baby?"

"Yes," she admitted.

"Camille, maybe we should wait awhile. I mean, I think that we started having problems when you got pregnant. Remember?"

"I know," she said. "But, this time, it will be different. Now I know that you love me. Plus, this time I really want a baby. The last time, I wasn't so sure."

"Babe," he said gently. "I know that a baby is what you think you want right now. But, I feel that we should take some time to make the decision together." He stared into her disappointed face. "Camille, I don't want what happened last time to happen again. I think that it's very important for the two of us to get some type of help."

"You mean like marriage counseling?" she asked.

"Yes. I know it won't hurt us. Then, once we're able to put all the hard feelings, disappointments, heartache and pain behind us, then we can start thinking about having another baby."

Camille sighed. "You know, Dexter, you are right. It's just that, I feel so- so empty inside. Losing my baby was the worst kind of pain," she admitted to him.

"Well, what do you think it did to me?" Dexter's eyes clouded over. "You're not the only one who's lost a child. I'm hurting too. That baby was just a much a part of me as it was of you. Just because I wasn't carrying it, doesn't mean that I didn't love it."

Camille stared at her husband. She saw so much written on his face. At that moment she knew that she didn't have to suffer alone anymore. The two of them could share their grief together.

"I have been so selfish," she told him. "I've been holding everything inside, because I felt that you wouldn't understand. And all along, you're feeling the same exact emotions that I'm feeling."

"I guess it's my own fault. I've shut you out. Most of my life, I've shut everybody out. It's a defense mechanism."

"But, I'm your wife, Dexter. We're supposed to be here for each other. It's okay for you to let me in."

"I know that now," he replied. "So many times, when you were trying to communicate your feelings to me, I put up a wall. I know that must have hurt you." He took her hand in his. "Can you ever forgive me? I'm going to work on opening up more."

"Is that a promise?"

"Yes, it's a promise."

"Dexter?" She stared at him suggestively.

"Yes?"

"Even though we're going to wait on making another baby, do you think it'll be okay for us to at least practice?"

"No, it's not okay. I don't have any protection," he told her.

"Like condoms?"

"Yeah, I'm a married man, I'd better not have nothing like that lying around here," he joked.

"True. But, I think the 7-Eleven on the corner carries that type of thing. Why don't you go get some?"

"Condoms? Man, I'm going to feel like a high school kid all over again. But, if this is what you want."

"It is." She watched him walk to the door. "Dexter?"

"Yes?" He turned and looked at her.

"I love you," she told him, staring into his eyes.

This time, Dexter didn't avoid her gaze or ignore her words. He stared back at his beautiful wife.

"I love you, too," he said thickly. She smiled. "See you in a little bit, baby."

"See you."

Chapter Thirty-Five

April felt pride for the first time in a long time. She'd just enrolled in college and was on her way to earning a degree in Business Management. She'd be the first person in her family to graduate, so she considered it a major accomplishment. She called Brittany.

"What's up?" Brittany sounded happier than she had in a long time. April knew that she'd been attending court ordered parenting classes and had met someone. Maybe he had something to do with her cheerfulness.

"I was just calling to see if you wanted to go out to celebrate?"

"What's the occasion?"

"I just enrolled in college," she told her with enthusiasm.

"You did what? Girl, that's great," Brittany enthused.

"Yes, I'll be starting the next session."

"I can't believe you're going to college," Brittany said in disbelief.

"I figured it's time. I'm not getting any younger."

"I know that's right. I have some good news myself," she admitted.

"Really? Well, spit it out."

"Reggie asked me to marry him."

"Brittany, that's the best news I've heard in a long time. You're engaged?"

"I know. I can't believe it. I finally found Mr. Right. He is the one." The excitement in her voice was contagious.

"I'm concentrating on my career and you're engaged to be married. It's your world, black girl," April teased.

"No, it's your world, Mrs. Career Woman."

They chatted for a while longer and decided to celebrate their good news at a restaurant called Texas Cattle Company. They had put their club hopping days behind them.

Brittany worked on being a better parent so that she could regain custody of her children. She'd sworn off clubs, drinking, and promiscuity and concentrated on what she needed to do. The state had placed her sons with her mother so at least she got to see them daily. She had been court ordered to attend parenting classes and once she completed her case plan, she could get her children back for good.

April had finally made a choice and turned Darren's name over to Child Support Enforcement. He finally got the message. At first, he'd been furious and had even stopped seeing his son. But, lately he'd started calling and coming to pick him up again. He'd even managed to get a job at a rental store delivering furniture. The last time he'd gotten DJ he'd brought him back with at least five name brand outfits and a pair of Air Jordans. He had finally turned into a real father.

April focused on being a better parent, too. She took more time out with her children, often taking them on family outings. She could see a big difference in her daughter. Peaches still sassed her, just not as often and she wasn't as disrespectful. April learned to talk to them instead of yell at them. It was still a day-by-day process. Being a single parent wasn't no easy task.

After she got off the phone with Brittany, April retrieved her purse. Her daughter had spent the weekend with her father and his wife. After they all sat down and discussed things, visitation rights had been agreed upon. Now, Alexis stayed with him every other weekend and certain holidays.

In the beginning April hadn't wanted to comply with the decision. She harbored resentment toward him because he'd denied his daughter for so many years. But, as time passed, she let it go. Eventually, she might even begin to like his wife. That would be far in the future, though.

She got into her pimped out ride and looked at her reflection in the review mirror. "You're the queen of your world, black girl," she said to herself. Then, she laughed aloud and turned on her music. She no longer went to clubs on a regular basis, but that didn't mean she couldn't rattle your windows with her bass. That's exactly what she did as she drove to Brittany's house.

Chapter Thirty-Six

*N*ot only did Brittany get her children back, she got herself a husband in the process. Even though the parenting classes that she'd attended had been court ordered, other parents voluntarily took them.

Reginald Donaldson, a recent divorcee who'd been awarded custody of his children, was there. During breaks, they would sit together and discuss all kinds of world issues. Soon, Brittany could sense something different and unique about Reggie. He was like no other man she'd ever met.

Reggie had seen through the pain and glimpsed Brittany's heart. He fell in love with the true person beneath the exterior. Two months later, he asked for her hand in marriage.

Brittany had never dreamed that she'd marry a deacon of a non-denominational church, but she'd left that up to Fate and God. At last, she'd finally discovered her self-worth and could love herself unconditionally. She didn't need a man's affection to feel validated anymore.

Epilogue

*I*t was one of the happiest days of Camille's life. One of her dearest friends would be married in a few minutes. She tried so hard not to cry because it might ruin her makeup, but it was quite difficult. She felt very emotional but for many different reasons.

A little over a year had passed since she'd met April Dillard and Brittany Anderson. They had grown close, especially throughout all the problems each of them had experienced individually.

She remembered when Brittany had flown into a fit of rage and bleached her ex-boyfriend's clothes. She'd even gone so far as to ram into the back of his car with her own. While trying to deal with the pain of getting over Craig, she had lost custody of her children. It hadn't been an easy time for her. But, all of that was in the past.

Now, her wedding day had arrived. They were in the church where her husband-to-be stood in as pastor every Sunday. Everything had been decorated so nicely. All the groomsmen and bridesmaids stood in place. Brittany had even regained custody of her sons and included them in the wedding. Her mother sat in the front row, beaming with pride.

As the pianist played the first chords of that familiar tune, "Here Comes the Bride," Camille continued to reminisce about the last few months.

April had dealt with her son father's lack of financial support. She'd continued to put up with a job that she hated until she'd finally had enough. Baby daddy got turned over to

216

Child Support Enforcement and she'd started sending out her resumes. She now worked at a marketing firm as a Procurement Specialist, making more than she ever had in her life. The company was also paying for her education.

Her own marriage had been touch and go for a while. She'd made some wrong decisions. She'd almost ended up losing Dexter, the best thing that had ever happened to her. But, they'd prevailed. After going through the tests, they'd come out on top.

She and Dexter had started attending marriage counseling and had eventually worked through their martial problems. More than a year had passed since she'd gone over the edge. With Dexter's love and continued support, she prayed she'd never slip again.

As she stood next to the other bridesmaids and watched Brittany glide down the aisle with confidence and looking radiant, tears of joy fell from her eyes. Brittany looked truly happy and beautiful, in her flowing white gown.

April, in her bridesmaid gown, looked adorable. She had met a nice young man who had attended the ceremony. They kept throwing smiles at each other. Who knew, maybe they'd be married next.

Camille remembered her own wedding and glanced at Dexter. He gave her one of his special smiles and mouthed the words, "I love you." She smiled back and blew him a kiss.

Brittany's wedding wasn't the only reason for Camille's happiness. Before she'd left the house she'd taken an EPT pregnancy test and it had been pink when she'd checked. She hadn't had an opportunity to tell Dexter yet. Her excitement over the news mounted. She couldn't wait.

They had just closed the deal on their new, four-bedroom, two and a half bath, house with a double garage located in

Lakewood Estates. It had an outside pool and an enclosed Jacuzzi. Their ideal home belonged to them. Now, her dreams would finally become a reality. She had her perfect husband, and soon, they'd have a precious child. She had friends who were there for her through thick and thin.

As she stood in the church, she realized just how truly blessed she was. Her friends loved her, and she them.

What about your friends?

EXCERPT FROM
PROJECT QUEEN II

BY TERESA D. PATTERSON

Chapter One

"Let's R. Kelly this bitch. Turn her over. Get a good picture, man. Zoom in on this."

Della, sprawled across the bed, felt nauseous. Downstairs, she heard her sister Shae arguing with her husband, Larry. It was most likely about her. Where ever she went, trouble always seemed to follow.

"Did you get a shot of that, man? Zoom in again. Turn that ass back around."

Della moaned aloud and held the sides of her head. "Stop," she said aloud. But, the voices wouldn't listen.

"St. Pete's Bitches Gone Wild! You heard?"

She remembered a lot of laughter and hands all over her body, touching...feeling...groping. Hot, heavy breathing, mouths, lips kissing and sucking her, tongues licking her. Her legs spread wide apart. Fingers thrusting in and out. Men on top of her. One, two then three of them...inside her.

"What the fuck?" She sat up and the room spun.

She tried, but couldn't remember much more. The events that had transpired the night before were groggy. She felt sick to her stomach. She stood up and winced when she felt a sharp pain between her legs.

"Ouch. Damn. What the hell happened to me last night?"

She'd been invited to a house party. She could recall talking and flirting with a guy named Paul. As the night progressed, they'd gone into a back bedroom. Afterwards, Paul left and the rest of them had continued to party and have a good time. Drinks had been made and Marijuana passed around. The rest of the night became a blur.

Even though she couldn't remember exactly what happened, it couldn't have been good. Not with the way she felt. It was like someone or something had probed all of her openings. There was a stinging sensation in both her vagina and anus. Her mouth even felt sore and bruised.

Shae and Larry's argument grew louder causing Della's head to throb. Why in the hell had she moved in with them? She knew it was time to find the next victim. Once again, she'd overstayed her welcome.

Two and a half years ago, she'd found out from her father, Jimmy Byrts, that she had sisters and brothers. Jimmy lived a secret life for many years. He didn't think it was important for her to know her siblings until he learned that his ex-wife had tried to kill them. The guilt forced him to come clean about it all.

Della hadn't wasted any time getting to know her siblings. Actually, she didn't give a shit about bonding or family ties. Her main intent was to use them as much as she could. Even though they'd grown up poor in the projects, they'd managed to make good lives for themselves. Vivian was a college professor and her husband a best-selling author. Shae was a bank manager, with a high-paid artist for a husband. Even Toby had money, though the way he made it wasn't conventional. He was known on the block as Big

Tobe. Whatever you needed to get high, he had it. If he didn't, he knew where to get it.

She victimized her oldest sister, Vivian, first. It worked for a while. She had it made, lounging around in Viv's huge, luxurious house, swimming in the heated pool, relaxing in the Jacuzzi, eating whatever she wanted, sleeping all day and fucking all night. She got too comfortable, thinking that she had Vivian and Richard wrapped around her finger. She had...until Vivian had caught her one time too many sneaking men out of her bedroom.

"Girl, you have got to go," Vivian told her the morning after she got busted entertaining two men in the outside Jacuzzi. One had his face buried between her thighs, and she was giving the other a blowjob. "I can't have you in my house, around my children, doing God knows what. I don't need them picking up on your bad habits."

"Viv," she whined. "Please. I won't do it anymore. I promise."

"No. I won't fall for it this time, Della. You have until the end of the week to move back with Jimmy, or find somewhere else to stay."

"Charles and Chris live with Jimmy. They have my old room." She pouted as if it would help her plead her case.

"That's not my problem." Vivian remained firm, not falling for the manipulation tactics. "Besides, Jimmy has a guest room. You can sleep there."

"But I don't want to live with Daddy. He's old fashioned. He won't let me do nothing," she complained.

"Like I said, it's not my problem. You are too hot in the ass. I don't like having strangers in my house. Even though I've told you that time after time, you keep bringing different men here. Look, I'm glad I got the chance to know you. You're not a bad person. You're just irresponsible, hard-headed, and too fast for your own good. You have worn out your welcome." She got ready to leave the room, but turned around. "And don't even think about trying to sweet-talk

Richard. We decided on this together. He's in agreement with me, and you won't be able to change his mind."

That's what she'd thought. Della knew exactly what to do about Richard. He was walking around with major blue balls because Vivian wasn't fucking him like she should. She could understand that her dear sister had to work and be a mother. Maintaining was hard, especially having twins and a toddler. But, Vivian left the door open for the clean-up woman to walk right in. Della was that clean up woman; stilettos, feather duster, fishnet stockings, hot pussy and all.

She found Richard in the den, sucked him off and rode his dick for over an hour. It allotted her another six months of sponging off her sister, rent-free.

Richard dicked her down on a regular basis so she didn't have to worry about being kicked out. The shit hit the fan when Vivian walked in on them one morning. They were getting busy on the bear-skinned rug in her bathroom. She thought Vivian was going to murder them on the spot. Instead, she threw them both out. From what Della heard, they were still trying to repair their marriage. No one in the family knew that she was the cause of the breakup. Vivian was too embarrassed to reveal it to anyone.

She shouldn't have stopped fucking him, Della thought. Of course she should feel some remorse because that was her sister, but she didn't. She was all about self and having her pussy purr.

She had no sympathy for Shae either. She'd fuck Larry in a heartbeat if he was even remotely interested. He all but ignored her when she flounced around him half-dressed. Shae had him pussy-whipped even though she treated him like shit.

She'd tried living with Jimmy after Vivian kicked her out, but she couldn't stand it. Jimmy treated her like a baby, not letting her go anywhere. When she did leave the house, she had a curfew. She didn't dare sneak anyone in after-hours because Jimmy would probably shoot first, and ask questions later. She just couldn't get fucked the way she wanted to with her father breathing down her neck all the time. If she did manage to invite someone over, Charles and Chris got in the way of anything popping off. She'd had to get away. She chose her next set of victims: Shae and Larry.

Della had no problem convincing most people to give her whatever she wanted. She was a bi-racial beauty, petite, with curves in all the right places. She had an amazing smile that could melt the coldest heart. She could be the sweetest person when she wanted to be, especially when she turned on the charm.

After hearing her sob story, of course Shae agreed to let her move in. Maybe she wanted to play big sister just like Vivian had. Della wasn't with that corny shit. Yes, they had the same daddy, but that wasn't enough to bond them. Plus, she'd be damned if she listen to Shae any more than she'd listened to Vivian. No one told her what she could and could not do. She'd ride the waves as long as the waters remained calm.

Once again, she lived high on the hog. Shae and Larry's house wasn't as luxurious as Vivian and Richard's. She couldn't expect everyone to have a Jacuzzi and heated pool. Shae and Larry's sadity asses had a swing set in the backyard. A freaking swing set—what black people put shit like that in their yards?

She'd just have to make do. At least she had her own room with an adjourning bathroom. Plus, she didn't have to come out her pockets with one red cent. She could live with that.

At first, things went smoothly and would have probably continued that way if Toby didn't live with them, too. He put his nose in her damn business, caught on to her late night encounters, and called her on them. She'd tried to win him over, but it hadn't worked. She'd even gone so far as to crawl into his bed and try to convince him that way. He'd slapped her so hard that she thought he'd broken her jaw.

"I'm your fucking brother bitch. You nasty, slutty ho. What the fuck is wrong with you? Don't ever try that shit again."

She remembered how angry Toby had been and laughed aloud. At least her brother had some morals and wasn't led by his dick. That was more than she could say about most men.

She didn't care what people thought of her. She would live her life the way she saw fit. If they didn't like it, they could kiss her ass. That included her family.

She found the remote to the stereo and turned it on, trying to block out Shae and Larry. She wished they'd shut the fuck up. Lately, all they did was argue.

Della had it figured out. Shae was bitchy all the time because Larry wasn't fucking her. Even though he presented himself as Mr. Straight and Narrow, he wasn't to be trusted. As long as he was a man, he was sure to have character flaws. She would bet her sexiest red thong that Larry was cheating.

Her headache persisted so she lay back down. Lester's twisted face floated behind her closed eyelids. Whatever happened to her, he'd been behind it.

She had to find out what went down at that party. She'd made a huge mistake hanging around Lester. He was a sleazy, crooked motherfucker. He'd been involved in all types of foul activity, including being a pimp. He even got arrested for messing around with under-aged girls, and had to register as a sex offender. His criminal record hadn't deterred him though. He still managed to convince gullible teens to give up the goods, offering them false promises of money and fame. He profited off of preying on the naïve and innocent.

She knew one thing: Lester better not have pulled any slick shit with her. If she ever found out he had, there would be hell to pay.

Chapter Two

How the fuck is she going to try me like this? Larry thought. There was a look of fury on his handsome face. He stared at Shae in disbelief as he pushed his plate to the side, appetite ruined by their argument. "I can't believe you'd accuse me of some shit like that, Shae. That's your baby sister. And she's a fucking child. What the hell would I want with a child?" He stood up to take his plate to the sink.

"She's damn near twenty, hardly a child. You haven't been fucking me lately, so you must be fucking somebody," Shae retorted.

"So, now I gotta damn-near be a pedophile on top of being a cheater?" He was so angry, he threw the plate at the sink, missing. The plate shattered and food fell to the floor, but he didn't care. He turned toward his wife, eyes flashing.

"Damn, Shae, what the fuck did I do to deserve this kind of treatment? I've been nothing but good to you and your brothers. And this is the thanks I get. You give me your ass to kiss. I swear-" He shook his head. "If it wasn't for Imani, I'd just pack up my shit and go."

"You're welcomed to do just that. Don't think that you have to stick around because of the baby. I'll do fine raising her on my own," she said angrily, grabbing the broom to sweep up his mess.

"You're a damn lie. I bet the first thing you'd do is run to the nearest child support office. It's all about you and what you want. It's always been like that and I'm sick of it."

"And I'm sick-"

Their conversation was interrupted when Toby charged into the house, slamming the door behind him.

"That's fucked up," he swore.

Larry and Shae headed into the living room, argument forgotten for the time being.

"What's wrong with you?" Shae asked.

Toby stood six-feet three. His was light in complexion with broad, buff shoulders and arms. It was obvious he worked out frequently. His handsome features were contorted with anger.

"That fucking sister of yours is a trifling, skank ass ho," he directed at Shae.

"What? Why would you say such a thing? You are talking about Della, right?"

"Yeah, I'm talking about her. Who else? She needs somebody to put their foot deep in her ass. You have to talk to her, Shae, and straighten her out."

"What did Della do now?" Larry just rolled his eyes and took a seat on the couch. He was still pissed at Shae for accusing him of being unfaithful.

"She's in this video called *St. Pete's Bitches Gone Wild.* Some nigga was selling the DVD's for ten dollars out of his trunk. That girl is getting buck wild, letting dudes run up in her, one after the next. It's just nasty. She needs to have some respect about herself. Now everybody in the streets talking about her like she's a dog. I don't even want nobody to know I'm some kin to her."

"And you honestly think I'd stoop that low and sleep with somebody like that?" Larry muttered, glaring at Shae.

"Hell nah. I don't believe Larry would touch Della with a donkey's dick. He might catch something," Toby said, chuckling.

Shae ignored Larry's comment. "What exactly do you think I should do about her?" she asked Toby. "She's out there. If she doesn't care about her reputation, why should I? She doesn't care about anything except having a good time. When she lived with Vivian, she had men in Vivian's house at all times of night. Viv had to put her out. Looks like I'm going to have to do the same thing."

"Either that or put your husband out," Larry implied, sarcastically. "It's not like you give your husband any credit.

Just because he has a dick, he must be fucking somebody on the side."

Toby laughed. "If you pulled that off Larry, you got all of us fooled. You 'bout the squarest nigga I know. I can't even picture you tipping. Hell nah."

"What are you trying to say, man?" Larry looked offended.

"Nothing. Shae is just tripping. You one of the last good brothers left. She better recognize."

The doorbell sounded. "Can one of y'all get that? I'm going upstairs to check on Imani," Shae threw over her shoulder, heading for the stairway.

"Make sure Della ain't up there doing nothing she shouldn't be," Toby tossed out. "Check for niggas up under the bed and in the closet. Man, that girl is off the chain. What's wrong with her?"

"I don't know. She better slow down before she catches something she can't get rid of," Larry mumbled, heading to answer the door. When he saw Jimmy Byrts standing there it didn't improve his mood. He knew Shae's attitude wasn't going to improve when she encountered her father.

"How are you, Mr. Byrts? Come on in," he invited.

"I'm doing fine. How about yourself?"

"I'm catching hell from my wife, but I'll keep my problems to myself." He indicated the couch. "Have a seat. Shae should be down in a minute."

"Hello Toby." Jimmy spoke to his son. Toby frowned, grumbled a muffled response and switched on the PlayStation. "You wanna play, Man?" He challenged Larry, ignoring his father

Larry threw Jimmy an apologetic smile. "I'll beat you anytime," he told Toby.

"How 'bout we put some money on it?"

"Man, if you really wanna lose your dough," Larry bragged. The two men soon became involved in the video game.

It wasn't long before Shae returned carrying Imani. When she saw that Jimmy had stopped by to visit she sucked air through her teeth in annoyance. She still couldn't stand her biological father. Even though he'd tried to be a part of her life for the last two and a half years, she wasn't softening toward him.

Imani, at age two, didn't have such reservations. She held her arms out for her grandfather.

"Grand DaDa," she called him and wiggled to get out of Shae's arms. She whined when Shae continued to hold on to her.

"Hey Pumpkin," Jimmy greeted just as enthusiastically. It was obvious that he loved his granddaughter. That didn't matter to Shae. He hadn't been there for her when she'd needed him. She'd suffered so many years of abuse because of his desertion. She couldn't just forget and let it go.

"Shae, let her get down," Larry said, watching Imani struggle and hold out her arms for her grandfather. Shae threw him a look of irritation, but did as he instructed. Imani immediately rushed over to Jimmy. He picked her up and swung her around causing Imani to laugh gleefully.

Shae turned away, swallowing down the lump in her throat. His swinging Imani around brought back a vision of him swinging her and Vivian around in a similar fashion. She didn't want to remember anything good about him. Her lips twisted.

"What do you want, Jimmy?" she snapped.

"Shae, don't be that way," Larry said noticing the sad look that crossed Jimmy's face.

"Don't tell me how to be with my father. Stay out of this," she snapped.

"I'm not going to take too much more of your disrespect, Shae. I love you, but I'll be damned if I continue to let you walk all over me," he retorted. "I don't deserve it."

Shae threw him a surprised looked. Larry never got bent out of shape. He usually just went along with whatever she wanted.

"Is something going on that I should know about?" Jimmy asked, staring from one to the other.

"It's your bad ass seed that's causing all the friction," Toby tossed in. "Speaking of the devil-" Della chose that moment to come downstairs.

"Hey Daddy," she greeted happily when she saw Jimmy and went to give him a hug. Shae rolled her eyes, feeling a tinge of jealousy at the affection the two shared.

"Della, what did you do?" Jimmy asked.

"I didn't do anything, Daddy." She stuck her lips out in a pout. "I don't know what's going on. When I woke up, they were arguing." She widened her eyes trying to appear innocent.

Toby just smirked at her and shook his head. "Why are you here old man?" he asked Jimmy, frowning at his father. "Just because you know where we live, don't mean you're invited over."

Jimmy cleared his throat. "I really need to talk to you...all of you."

"This sounds serious. I'll take Imani outside to play on the swings and leave y'all to it," Larry said, picking up his daughter. "Come on, baby girl." They left the room, giving the family some privacy.

"What's wrong, Daddy?" Della asked. If she had a caring bone in her body, it was for her father. "You don't look so good. Toby, can you get him something to drink?"

"What's wrong with your legs?" he snapped, scowling at her.

"Fine. I'll get it," Della snapped back, heading for the kitchen.

"Della's right. You don't look so good," Shae said.

Sweat poured down the sides of Jimmy's face and beads of perspiration stood out on his forehead. He stared at Shae then Toby. Both of their faces were formidable. He cleared his throat and waited for Della.

When Della returned with a glass of water, Jimmy took it gratefully.

"Thanks, baby girl." He swallowed some and placed the glass on a coaster in the middle of the table.

"Talk ol' man," Toby said impatiently. "I got things to do. Time means money."

"This is hard for me." Jimmy sat up and laced his fingers together. "As you all know, I had a serious drinking problem. It was the main reason that me and your mother couldn't get along." This was directed at Shae and Toby. "I drank heavily for many years. Well, now it's affecting my health." He inhaled deeply and let it out slowly. "I need a liver transplant."

"What?" Della asked in shock, her voice trembling. "Are you going to die, Daddy?"

"No. No, I'm not going to die," he said reassuringly. "I've been on a waiting list. They have a liver for me. I just need a blood transfusion."

"Why?" Shae couldn't stop the question from slipping past her lips. Her eyes met Toby's. She knew that he wanted to hear the answer too even though he was pretending like he didn't care.

"During the operation, I may lose blood so that blood needs to be replaced."

"How do they replace it?" Della asked. Her eyes were wide and transfixed on her father.

"They'll do it through an IV. They will just replace the blood I've lost with healthy blood," he explained. "It's nothing major."

"How do we find out if we're a match?" Shae asked.

"You'll just go in and let them prick your finger. Once they find out if your blood type matches mine, we can proceed from there," he relayed the information that he'd received from his doctor.

Toby leaped up, his eyes blazing. "You better hope that I'm not a match 'cause if I am, ya ass is as good as dead," he said. "Sorry for breaking up this Brady Bunch moment, but I'm out."

"I understand why you feel that way," Jimmy said, reaching for Toby's arm causing him to flinch. "At least think about it. Call me and let me know your decision."

"I already told you," Toby growled, pulling away from his father's touch. A hurt expression flickered across Jimmy's face.

"Toby, stop," Shae said. She felt a small amount of sympathy for her father. He suddenly looked old and frail. They'd missed so many years and now, they might not have too many more left to spend with him. "We'll call you," she assured him.

Jimmy threw her a grateful smile. "I'll go find Imani to say good-bye." He got up and made his way out of the room, walking like a doomed man.

"Why the hell would I want to give him my blood?" Toby exploded. "That nigga ain't never gave me shit." His face tightened. "He left us with Mama in them broke down, rat-infested ass projects. He didn't even send a damn dime in child support. Can you believe that shit? We lived worse than fucking cockroaches, in the projects, and all the while, we had a daddy who didn't give a shit about us. We got our asses stomped on a daily basis, and he didn't care. Our mama tried to kill us. Did he do anything to stop that?" He shook his head. "Now, this motherfucker wants one of us to save his life? Whatever."

For a moment, silence enveloped the room. Shae stared down at the floor. Della's expression was unreadable.

Della finally spoke. "It shouldn't matter. He's still your father," she said.

"What the fuck you mean, it shouldn't matter?" He glared at her. "You weren't there. You didn't have to go through the shit we went through. Since you don't know what went down, shut the fuck up," Toby growled.

"My childhood wasn't all peaches and cream either," Della tossed back. "But Jimmy took me in and saved my life. He's a good person and he's trying to be a better father." She could tell Toby wasn't moved by her words. She rolled her eyes at him. "I hope I'm a match. If I am, I'll give him my blood."

Toby threw her a look of disdain. "The way you been tricking all over the hood, your blood might be tainted. If he ain't dead yet, he *will be* using your contaminated shit," he insulted.

"What are you talking about, Toby?"

"Like you don't know." Toby smirked at her, remembering the tape he'd glanced at briefly. She was Little Red Getting Rode in the Hood. His lips twisted in disgust.

"Both of y'all stop," Shae intervened. "We'll just have to find out if we're a match. We'll take it from there. Will you at least do that, Toby? Like Della said, he is our father, and he's been trying to be involved in our lives now. I have to admit, he's wonderful with Charles, Chris and Imani. They seem to love him."

"Shit." Toby hesitated. His twin brothers did love Jimmy. They'd taken to him straight away. It was easy for them to do since they were so young. They hadn't been born when he left, so they didn't have a father to miss all those years. He, on the other hand, had major reservations and tons of resentment.

"Come on Toby," Shae pressed. "We can't let him die."

Toby seemed deep in thought. "Hell. Fuck it. I'll do it," he finally agreed. "Just let me know when and where. Now, I have to bounce for real. Love, peace, and hair grease." When he stood up they could see his boxers because his sagging pants hung below his waist.

"Toby, pull your pants up. I thought you'd outgrown that phase," Shae complained.

"Shae, you ain't my mama. I'm seventeen-years-old. In case you forgot, I can wipe my own ass."

Della laughed and Shae gave her a sharp look.

"I don't know what you think is so funny," Shae told her. "You and I need to have a talk. Sit down." Della glanced at Toby as she took a seat on the couch.

I ain't Captain Save-a-Ho, he thought. *I don't want anything to do with the conversation.* He shrugged and headed for the door.

Shae's voice halted him. "Toby, don't even think about leaving."

"Damn." He went to sit back down, pulling up his pants in the process.

"Now, what is this I hear about you being on some tape?" Shae asked Della.

Della's mouth dropped open in shock. "What tape?"

"I don't know. That's why I'm asking you," Shae said firmly.

"I am not on any damn tape," Della denied.

"Yeah, you are. I saw you," Toby said.

"Saw me when? On what tape?" Her voice raised in anger. "Who the fuck got a tape with me on it 'cause I want to know?"

"Some nigga had a DVD *called St. Pete's. Bitches Gone Wild.* He was selling them for ten bones out his trunk. You-" He pointed at her "-are on it."

"What the fuck? I don't know anything about this. Where the nigga at?"

"He's probably still selling them in the parking lot at Flawless Car Wash off 18th Ave. and 28th St. S."

"I got to see this shit. I ain't agreed to do nothing in front of a camera," she said vehemently.

"I'll take you over there right now and you can see for yourself. That was you I saw, and it was some scandalous shit." They both got up and headed for the door.

"I guess we'll talk later," Shae called behind them. "Don't end up in handcuffs." From the set look on Della's face, somebody had some explaining to do.

Shae sighed. She remembered those days when she'd deemed herself the *"Project Queen."* She'd been involved in so much drama. She continuously fought both men and women, demanding to be respected. It took many years for her to learn that respect couldn't be beat from a person. It had to be earned.

She was guilty of using the different men in the hood for money or whatnot. Even though people gossiped about her, no man could claim that he'd slept with her. Only two men could truthfully say that. Those two men were Larry and Dana. Since Dana was dead, he'd never be able to tell a soul.

Larry had taken her virginity. She reflected back on that day and smiled. Thinking about the first time they made love softened her heart toward him. She couldn't stay mad at him.

Her husband was a sweetheart. He gave her everything she desired. He purchased a huge house in an upscale neighborhood. He bought her a luxurious car- the latest BMW. He even insisted that she keep the money she earned at the bank, because he took care of all the household expenses. He was an awesome father to Imani, spoiling her to no end. He worked hard and provided everything they needed. He loved his family and took great care of them.

She'd been unfair in her treatment of him lately. Since Della moved in with them, there'd been so much tension. She didn't really suspect that Larry had slept with Della. She trusted her husband, but she wouldn't put anything past her sister.

The last time she'd spoken to Vivian, she got the distinctive impression that Viv was hiding something. She would put money on Della being behind it. The girl was something else, and not in a good way.

Now, there was this business about some videotape. Della had a wild side and she loved to party. Maybe it was time for her to slow down.

Shae shook her head. She couldn't do anything about Della's issues. Della would have to handle them herself. She needed to concentrate on her own problems. She could no longer convince herself that she and Larry weren't headed for trouble. She had to talk to him and find out what was on his mind.

She followed her daughter's giggles and found them in the backyard. Larry was pushing Imani on the swing. He'd hired professionals to fix their backyard into a child's play area. There was a swing set, sandbox, slide and even a merry-go-round. He often played with Imani there and wanted to have a pool installed when she got older.

"Is Jimmy gone?" she asked, walking up to stand next to him.

"Yes. He left about a half hour ago."

"Larry." She hesitated. It was hard for her to apologize, but she really didn't want to push her husband away. "I'm sorry about the way I've been acting. I know you would never cheat on me, especially not with my sister."

"Really?" Larry seemed uninterested, his jaw tight with anger.

"Larry, don't be mad." She slipped her arms around him. "I love you." Even though he continued to push Imani on the swing, she felt him relax.

"Nice way of showing it," he said, pouting.

"I've just been under a lot of stress and that hot ass sister of mine don't help things one bit. She prances around you all the time, half dressed, twisting and jiggling. It's obvious that she's flirting. There's no shame in her game."

"So you think she's going to attract me like that because that's how you caught me?" Larry asked.

"What?" She glanced at him, perplexed.

"You remember how you used to wear them little skirts, and booty shorts? That's how you caught me." He gave her a sly smile.

"Oh really?" Her brow rose.

"Um hum. That day you and I did it for the first time you were wearing something tight and provocative. I remember."

"I don't remember you complaining."

"I was mesmerized. You had me so hypnotized with that booty goin' 'round and 'round," he teased.

Shae laughed. "Whatever.".

"You think Viv wouldn't mind babysitting?" he asked.

"I'll call her and ask. Why?"

"I want an uninterrupted night alone with my wife."

"I like the sound of that. Don't ask for more than you can handle," she said lowly, licking her lips.

"Oh, I can handle it. Girl, you might need a back brace after tonight. Cause, I'm gonna knock it out," he bragged.

"Okay. We'll just have to see about that." She smiled.

They gazed into each other's eyes, the love and passion rekindled. Larry leaned over, capturing her lips with his own.

"I love you. Don't ever forget that."

How could she ever forget? He'd proven how deep his love was when he'd killed a man for her.

Chapter Three

Toby sat in his Cadillac Escalade and waited for Della to handle her business. He didn't want to get involved in her mess unless he had to. While she confronted the man about the DVDs, he counted his money. No one could see inside the dark limo-tinted windows.

Stackin' papers, that's what I'm about, he said to himself. He looked at all the money in his lap and littering the seat, and sighed. It was said that the love of money was the root of all evil and he had to agree.

His evil ass mother had tried to kill her family because of her love for money. Some three years later, he still couldn't understand why Bertha had tried to poison him, his brothers and sister. He felt that the constant abuse she'd inflicted on him and his siblings had been unnecessary. They had been powerless to do anything about it.

To this day, he still felt powerless about a lot of things, but no one would ever be able to look at him and tell. All of his money represented power. It gave him respect. In the hood, you couldn't be lame and weak or you'd get squashed.

He thought he'd be able to turn his life around, go back to school and make it out the hood the right way. But, in the hood, it doesn't work like that. You're either in the game or you're lame. It's just that simple.

All of his friends dibbled and dappled in drugs to some extent. No matter how he tried, he couldn't stay away from the lifestyle. Plus, it was easy money. He didn't have to hunt for drug addicts – they found him. If he wasn't the one selling them the poison they craved, somebody else would.

He wasn't proud of being one of the top drug dealers in the city. So far, he'd gotten by on luck. No one had attempted to rob him. He didn't count the strung-out crack heads that got lucky and took off with a rock without paying for it. That was comical to him and he didn't even bother to give chase. He figured they needed the hit more than he needed the chunk change.

He knew of cats that had gotten taken out. They lost their lives behind drugs and shady dealings. He felt it was only a matter of time before something happened to him, especially with it being a recession. Hell, when wasn't it a recession for black folk? Everyone was desperate, down and out. He really needed to watch his back.

Just the other week, a guy named Levi who used to go to school with him was murdered. His body was found in a dumpster, burned beyond recognition. He couldn't believe someone did that to Levi. But, Levi had gotten addicted to crystal meth and crack. He'd fucked over the wrong person, owed them money and couldn't pay. It was sad and it sent a message to him. He needed to do something other than sell drugs. Unlike Levi, he wanted to live past the age of nineteen.

Maybe an angel was looking down on him and protecting him. They say God looks out for babies and fools. Then again, it could be Ma Violet. Whoever it was that had his back, he owed it to them to turn his life around.

Lately, he'd been thinking about giving it all up. It wasn't like he needed the money. Maybe when he was younger, it gave him a rush. Now, it did nothing for him.

He was tired of niggas looking at him sideways, and women trying to offer him some ass just because he had money. It was all a façade. If he wasn't Big Tobe, he knew no one would even be checking for him but his family. It was time for a change.

He exhaled and looked out the window. The conversation between Della and the guy seemed to be getting heated. It was time for him to intervene. He slipped a Beretta 9 mm handgun in the waist of his pants, and prayed he wouldn't have to use it.

* * *

Della felt an explosion in her brain as she watched the DVD in front of her. It *was* her on the screen. The men were pawing her like she was a piece of meat. The footage was extremely vulgar and explicit. She couldn't remember doing the things that the vixen was doing, but apparently she *had*. The video was proof.

In a blink of an eye, she snatched the portable DVD player and smashed it to bits on the concrete.

"What the fuck you doing, bitch? That's my shit." The street vendor tried to stop her from destroying the player, but it was too late. "You gonna pay for that," the trunk salesman snapped, looking at the pieces left.

"Motherfucker, I'm not paying you shit." She kicked the broken parts for emphasis. "Fuck you."

"The hell you ain't." He grabbed her by the arm, shaking her. She snatched away and slapped him hard across the face.

"Keep your hands off me, nigga."

"You can't just fuck up my shit and think I ain't gonna do nothing about it," he yelled.

"Nigga, I'll fuck you up, too," she said.

The man drew back his arm, preparing to backhand slap her, but Toby stepped in.

"Hold up," he warned, towering above the man who cowered as soon as he saw Toby. "That's my sister you're manhandling." The man quickly released Della.

"My bad. She destroyed my shit." He indicated the broken DVD player scattered in pieces on the ground. Toby shrugged indifferently.

Della was about to go off. Her entire face was red, and her eyes bloodshot with anger.

"I wanna fuck somebody up. Anybody," she screamed. She suddenly hauled off and kicked the passenger's side door of the man's car.

"Stop that. That's vandalism." The man was flouncing around like a chicken, his face flushed "You can go to jail for doing that."

"You think I give a fuck?" Della raged. "I want to know where you got those DVDs." By then she'd made her way to the front of the car, where she beat on the hood. She grabbed the windshield wipers and broke one of them off. "Tell me." She took a swing at him with the windshield wiper blade.

"Get her, man," the guy begged, looking toward Toby with fear in his eyes.

"Tell us where you got those DVDs," Toby said, ignoring him. "Start talking fast. You feel me?"

"Big Tobe, I-I-I don't want no mess," he stammered. "I don't know what's going on. I'm just trying to make a living." He took a step back, looking like he would piss in his pants at any given second. "I'm a reformed drug addict. I stopped smoking that shit and tried to get a job. But, you know ain't nobody gonna hire me. So, I gotta do what I do to make it, man."

"I don't give a shit about your life history, nigga. Just tell me where you got these DVDs," Toby repeated, feeling the rage trying to surface. He hated when niggas tried to give him a sob story about the so-called hard lives they'd led. Hell, he'd lived a hard life too. He had the scars on his back to prove it. He had no sympathy for weak niggas like this crack head lying to his face about being reformed. He could bet if he pulled out a ten dollar rock, the crusty-lipped bastard would be all on it and hitting the pipe in mere seconds.

"I got 'em from a nigga named Lester; ex-pimp, turned hustler."

"I know the nigga you talking about," Toby said.

"He gave me a deal. I bought a hundred at a discount price. I figured I'd sell them for ten dollars and make a profit. Hell, I didn't know it was ya sister on the tape. I ain't even look at it. I swear. I don't watch porn."

Toby just smirked at him. The nigga was an awful liar. "Consider yourself out of business." Toby walked toward the trunk and the man attempted to block his way with his thin body.

"This is my livelihood. If you don't work, you don't eat," he said pleadingly.

"Nigga, I know yo' crack smoking ass ain't trying to quote scriptures at me. Step yo' lame ass back," Toby instructed, giving him a slight push. He grabbed the box of DVD's, glaring at the man. "You're lucky I don't bust a cap in yo' ass, nigga." He lifted his shirt, showing the butt of the Beretta then let his shirt fall back into place. "You know of anybody else selling these?"

"Nah." The man shook his head nervously. "Lester said he was copying some mo', and told me to holla at him if I ran out."

"Fuck nigga." Della gave the man a swift kick in the balls, and he doubled over in pain. "You'll think twice before you ever agree to sell anything with my face in it." She slapped him up-side-the head with the broken windshield wiper.

"Ouch. Stop hitting me," the man whined, drawing up in fear. "Get her, man. She's crazy."

Toby laughed and pulled Della in the direction of the Escalade. "Come on. Let's go find that motherfucker Lester."

"When we do find him, I'm gonna fuck him up," Della fumed.

***

They drove around looking for Lester, searching all the places he usually frequented. The snake had slithered back under a rock because they couldn't find him anywhere.

"I'm going in here to get me something to drink," Toby told Della as he pulled into a parking space at Ike's Liquor Lounge. Even though he was underage, the manager of the store knew him. Toby had money to burn, so they sold him whatever he wanted, no questions asked.

Toby went inside the store and Della remained behind listening to Lil Wayne rapping on a new single. Even though he seemed to be on everybody's CD, just like T-Pain, she didn't mind. Unlike T-Pain, Lil Wayne could rap. She sang along with the song, laughing at the lyrics.

I like a long haired thick red bone.
Open up her legs to filet mignon.

She wondered how Lil Wayne came up with some of his lyrics. She'd heard that he free styled and didn't write any of his stuff down.

Cuz we like her
and we like her too.

She felt someone staring at her and glanced over at the chick. She was a brown-skinned woman, wearing a two-toned, purple and black, hair weave. Not recognizing the girl, she looked away. The girl kept mean-mugging her so she reacted the best way she knew how; with attitude.

"What the fuck are you looking at?" Della snarled.

"I'm looking at you. Ain't you in that video circulating around? You look just like that girl."

"I don't know what you're talking about." Della wanted to sink down in the seat and hide.

So, the video is out there and people qre watching it. Now, they'll recognize me. Damn Lester to hell!

"I bet." The girl smirked. "You look just like that light-skinned bitch on there sucking dicks and doing all kind of other nasty shit. It's called *St. Pete.'s. Bitches Gone Wild.* That's not you in it?"

"Bitch, I *said* I don't know what you're talking about," Della repeated, getting loud.

"I know you not getting salty, ho. You feeling froggy, then leap," the girl egged her on, obviously drunk with courage.

"Who the fuck you calling a ho?"

"You, ho. Skanky ass dirty slut."

"Bitch, if I get out this truck, you best believe you'll be wearing an ass whipping," Della warned. The girl just rolled her eyes and curled her lips in disgust.

"If that was you on that tape them niggas dogged yo' ass out. You got exactly what you deserved, too. 'Cause you got a fucked up ass attitude, bitch."

Della was out of the Escalade in a flash, leaping on the lady like cat woman. As she rode the woman's back like she was a bronco, she snatched hands full of hair weave out of her scalp. The woman just screamed and tried to buck Della off.

"Get her off me," she screamed. "She's fucking up my hair-do."

Toby came out the liquor store. Seeing what was going on, he shook his head. He decided to let Della relieve some of her frustrations for a minute.

After putting his purchases in the truck, he walked over and pulled Della off the girl. Everybody else just stood around cheering and egging the fight on.

"Bitch, I'mma fuck you up," the girl who'd just received the ass whipping of her life, yelled. Tracks from her weave job lay in clumps on the ground. Some of her acrylic nails were broken to the cuticle. "I just got my fucking hair done. Damn."

"Let me go Toby. I wanna fuck that bitch up bad. I wanna cut her fucking face off." Della pulled out a straight-edge razor, like one they use at barber shops to shave customers.

"Whoa. Put that shit away and get in the truck before you end up going to jail," Toby said.

"I don't give a fuck. I'll carve that ho up. I'll slice that bitch's lips off. She won't be able to talk shit, then." Della trembled with anger.

"Della, come on," Toby urged. "Get your ass in the truck so we can get the fuck out of here." Toby picked her up and pushed her into the passenger's seat of the SUV. He got in and sped off, putting the pedal to the metal.

Della fumed. She closed the weapon and put it away. She curled up in the seat and began to rock back and forth.

"What the fuck is wrong with you, girl?" Toby yelled. "I leave you alone for a hot minute and you start some shit. You fucking with people that I know. Them my motherfucking customers. You stand a chance of staining my rep. I can't have that shit. You better tell me something." She continued to rock. "Stop doing that. You're acting like a crack head, rocking and shit." Della continued to rock and it annoyed him. "Stop doing that," he repeated.

"I can't-"

"Yes, you can. Sit still right now," he demanded.

It took a minute, but Della finally pulled herself together. She still had her arms crossed over her breasts, but she'd ceased rocking.

"Now tell me what was you and that bitch fighting about?"

"She said something that I didn't like."

"What do you expect?" Toby asked in exasperation. "Huh? You go around fucking any and everybody. You end up getting recorded. People are gonna talk shit."

"She said I deserved it." She suddenly burst into tears. "But, I didn't deserve that. I didn't deserve it, Toby."

"What are you talking about?" Toby hoped his sister wasn't having a mental break down. He'd heard about mental illness running in the family, but Della had a different mama than him.

"What they did to me on that tape. She said I deserved it." She was crying so hard that he could barely understand her. "I didn't even- I didn't."

"Calm down and take a deep breath," he suggested. "We're almost home."

"Just because I agreed…to let one man fuck me, doesn't mean…I deserved to be drugged and raped," she finally managed to get out.

"Who drugged you?" Toby tried to let what she'd said sink in. "And who the fuck raped you?" He felt the blood rush to his head.

"That motherfucker Lester must have put something in my drink." After fighting with the woman at Ike's Liquor Lounge, everything came back to her. She remembered the details of that night clearly.

"Hold up. Hold up. Tell me everything from the beginning," Toby commanded so she did. Toby's face hardened as she spoke. But she hadn't gotten to the worse part.

"I know you think I'm a slut and a whore. I'm not. I just like sex a lot, and I'm freaky. But, even I draw the line at having niggas run trains on me and nutting all in my face. That shit is nasty and degrading. And did you see what else they did to me?"

"Hell nah," he stated quickly. "I couldn't watch that shit. When I recognized that it was you, I stopped looking. Don't nobody wanna see their sister getting ran through and dogged out." His lips curled in distaste.

"Well, I'll tell you what they did." She stared at him with a crazed look in her eyes. "They fucked me in the ass. Fucked me until I shitted all over myself." Her eyes darkened with hatred as she remembered.

"Aw damn!" Toby hit the steering wheel with the palm of his hand. "Fuck!"

"I want to kill the motherfuckers," she said with venom in her voice.

"I don't fucking blame you." He just shook his head, still shocked by what she'd shared.

"Toby, I know I put myself in a bad situation. But, what they did to me wasn't right. And to think them entreponegros are profiting off of it, that makes my blood boil."

Toby pulled into the driveway. They sat in silence for a while. All that could be heard was Della's sniffles.

"We can't get rid of the tapes that are already out there," he finally said. "But we can stop that motherfucker from selling anymore of 'em."

"You gonna help me?"

"Shit, I hate to think about what happened to you. It's foul. You didn't deserve that. No woman does." He ran his hands over his eyes. "I'll take care of it."

"And Toby-"

"Yeah?"

"I'm sorry about what I did," she said in a small voice. She had a faraway look in her eyes, as she stared at nothing. "You know, when I snuck into your bed and tried to-"

"Girl, don't ever bring that shit up again," Toby said vehemently. "Never, no more in this lifetime." He shivered in disgust.

"I can't help it, Toby. It's the only way I know how to show love." She felt ashamed remembering how she'd tried to perform oral sex on her own brother. What was wrong with her?

He was silent for a moment then said, "Well, maybe you need to get some help for that. I mean, you can't just go around sleeping with everybody. It's dangerous. You see what ended up happening."

A look of sadness flickered across his face. It really bothered him that men he knew could violate his sister like that. He hadn't known her for that long, but blood was still thicker than water.

"Sometimes, I feel like killing myself," she said softly.

Her words stabbed him in the heart. "Don't talk like that, D. Ain't nothing so bad that you have to end your life over it." He reflected back on those dismal days of living in the projects, being mentally and physically beat down daily by his mother. He'd felt so hopeless, but he'd never thought about taking his own life.

He glanced at his sister. She was rocking back and forth again. He just shook his head. He didn't have the heart to tell her to stop after hearing her story. There was more to Della than she cared to share. What kind of life had she led? From the little that he knew, she hadn't always lived with Jimmy.

"That video is all over St. Pete. Everybody's going to see it. I can't let that happen." Desperation crept into her voice. "We have to find Lester."

"That motherfucker Lester will be dealt with. Believe that," Toby promised. "Go inside. I have some business to take care of."

"What are you gonna do, Toby?"

"Don't worry about it. Just go in the house," he insisted.

"Don't get into trouble because of me. I'll take care of Lester and the rest of those motherfuckers, too. I won't breathe easily until I've paid each and every one of them back," she said evenly. "Mark my words, Toby. Payback is going to be a bitch."

* * *

Toby drove around, mind heavy with thoughts. He knew that he had to be careful in how he handled Lester once their paths crossed. And their paths *would* cross. Lester would have to be held accountable for his actions. He couldn't just get away doing foul shit and not have to suffer any consequences.

His thoughts switched to Della. He could easily blame what happened to her on her whorish ways, but he couldn't. He sensed her problems ran deeper than that. She put herself out there, but those niggas crossed the line when they drugged her and ran through her like Amtrak. They were stupid enough to keep evidence, too- and bold enough to sell the damn video.

Niggas just weren't too bright. They had that "Burg mentality." They had to dumbly showcase the shit they did, and brag about it. Didn't they know that what's done in the dark always makes it to the light?

He was so glad he didn't think like a typical nigga. He'd never take what wasn't his. Hell, even if it was offered, he turned it down. How could they just drug a woman and force her to do all kinds of things she wouldn't normally do? Then tape it all? What did they think: that it wouldn't get back to her?

Della wasn't a bad person. She was just misguided. She wanted to be loved and accepted and was going about it the wrong way. He was shocked at the amount of men she messed around with. She really didn't seem to care about herself or value her body.

He remembered the time she'd tried him. She'd been living with them for about three months. Shae and Larry went to bed at a decent our, so they had no clue what Della was up to. Toby knew that she snuck men in the house frequently. He'd witnessed it quite a few times and wasn't cool with it at all.

First, he had a three-year-old niece that he was concerned about. If any nigga fucked with her or tried some sick shit, he would be doing life behind bars. He didn't know the men and thought Della needed to keep her activities out of their home environment.

Next, he worried about them trying to rob him. They might be out to get him and used Della for easy access. It could happen.

His mind was constantly coming up with different scenarios, keeping him on edge. He didn't feel comfortable with strange people invading his personal space.

One night he decided to tell Della exactly what was on his mind. Of course, she didn't see any problem with her actions.

"Toby, I'm grown. I know you don't expect me to be a nun."

"I expect you to have some self-respect and decency about yourself," he said.

"That's like the pot calling the kettle black. What about you, Toby? You're a big-time dope boy. You got a lot of self-respect and decency?" she asked sarcastically. "You have some nerve to look down on me."

"I'm not looking down on you. I'm just worried. We don't know the people you bring in here. What if they are pedophiles or something? Think about Imani."

"Stop trying to be my daddy," she snapped. "Nothing is going to happen to Imani. I won't let it."

"I won't either. That's why you gonna stop sneaking niggas in this bitch," he informed.

"You can't tell me what to do."

"If you don't stop, I'll tell Shae and Larry. They won't be too happy knowing what you've been up to. You'll be packed and back at Jimmy's in a heartbeat."

"Whatever." She flounced off in anger.

Later that night he felt someone crawl into his bed. He thought he was dreaming. When he felt the sheet slide from his body, his eyes popped opened. He felt a hand reaching down into his boxers. He snapped wide awake and jumped out of the bed.

"What the fuck are you doing?" he yelled. It was Della. Apparently, she was trying to get with him in the wrong way.

"Can't we keep what's been going on between us?" Della asked, trying to sound sexy. "If you don't tell Shae and Larry, I'll make it worth it."

"What the hell are you talking about?"

"You know. I can show you better than I can tell you." She dropped to her knees in front of him and grabbed his crotch.

That's when he slapped her. "I'm your fucking brother, bitch. You nasty, slutty ho. What the fuck is wrong with you? Don't ever try that shit again."

He shivered in disgust remembering that incident. He hadn't meant to lose it and slap the shit out of her. It had been a reflex action. He wanted her to know that he meant business. He wasn't the type of low-life that fucked his own sister. That was sick.

Della got it together after that. He didn't see anymore strangers coming in and out, and he could breathe more easily. She still liked to hang out late and party, but that was her prerogative. He couldn't tell her what to do. As long as she wasn't disrespecting him or putting the rest of them in danger, it was her life.

Now, some niggas had taken things too far. They'd disrespected his sister in the worse way and he would have to handle it. He wasn't a ruthless nigga like Dana used to be, but he did have a dark side. Unfortunately, Lester was going to experience it.

Della might not be wrapped too tight. She might even be considered a slut, but she was still his sister. And you don't fuck with his family. Period.

ABOUT THE AUTHOR

TERESA D. PATTERSON is the author of Project
Queen, Uncrossing Her Legs, Ex-boyfriend, In Need of
a Joshua Man and Spin Cycle. She is the founder of Edit
Again Publications. She resides in Florida with her two
sons, where she continues to write.

Website: www.teresadpatterson.com
Email: teresadpatterson@yahoo.com

www.ingramcontent.com/pod-product-compliance
Lightning Source LLC
Chambersburg PA
CBHW011520240626
47154CB00009B/2905